FAMILY SECRETS

NICOLE K. HORN-SHELTON

ISBN: 978-1-7366711-1-5

Email: authornicolehornshelton@gmail.com

Website: nicolehornshelton.com

I would like to dedicate this book to the loving memory of my parents; Marilyn and Robert Tate, my grandmother, Anna Horn and my Godfather, Kevin Majett. I hope I am making you all proud. I miss you all so much. Keep shining your light so I can see my way through.

To:
Brian Nero
Thank you for your
support. Many Blessings
upon you.

Author Nicole Henry Shute

August 20, 2022

PROLOGUE

"Shoot him!"

I froze staring at the man before me. For some reason he didn't look scared. I look nervously around the room. There were six other men standing there with guns in their hands. The room seemed to spin as I held this man's fate in my hands. The cold steel of the gun made me feel powerful but at that moment I wasn't sure if I could take a life. My victim was kneeling on a large piece of thick plastic with his head up and chest out, letting me know he was not afraid. He refuses to die like a coward. My inner thoughts consume me, as time seemed to stand still. I could literally hear my heart pulsating against my chest.

"If you want to be a boss then shoot him now!" he shouts.

A tear rolled down my face...POW! The sound of the shot echoed loudly in my ear. His body fell right in front of me with blood pouring from his forehead. As I stared down at his lifeless body, I noticed his eyes were twitching. My heart skipped a beat, and my hands began to shake uncontrollably as the gun slipped from my fingertips.

—————————————————

The sight of his dead body jolts me from my deep slumber as the sweat pours through my skin. *Okay. Get it together. Shake that shit off.* I can't believe I'm still having recurring nightmares after four years. Of course I can't tell anyone about this because they will think I'm weak. I have no choice but to figure out how to deal with this on my own. Something I've had to do for far too long. For now, I'll just get ready for school. I quickly hopped out of bed, took a hot steamy shower to try and clear my thoughts of that damn nightmare. A nightmare that finds it's way into my dreams no matter how hard I try to avoid them. After my quick shower, I grab a pair of black leggings with an oversized off the shoulder black and white sweater. I slid on my red, black, and white Jordans. I didn't feel like putting on heels today. That nightmare has put me in a foul mood.

As I was walking down the hall about to go to lunch, I hear loud shouting and screaming.

"They're fighting! They're fighting!"

I follow the crowd to the action and see the new girl, Irie fighting with Samantha. Irie transferred to our school last year, I knew it would be hard for her here—everyone grew up together and never welcomed newcomers. I knew this day would come because I kept hearing rumors about her. They constantly talked about what she wore and how she looked. They were extremely jealous of her. Today she wore Balenciaga sneakers and diamond hoop earrings. Irie Clarke is a full-blooded Jamaican with long dreads, a banging body, cute, and chocolate. Don't let her cute looks fool you.

I run to where the fight is as the new girl beats the shit out of Samantha, provoking two of Samantha's friends to jump in. Irie didn't skip a beat. She fought them off like a pro, until they started getting the best of her. I usually mind my business, but I wasn't about to let that go down. I jumped in to help the new girl and we beat the shit out of them.

Once Irie and I finished handling Samantha and her

friends, I helped Irie gather herself, the three of them laid out on the floor as teachers finally decided they wanted to break shit up.

"Yo! I appreciate you helping me. I wish those bitches would leave me the fuck alone. They can talk about me, I don't care, but that bitch Samantha walked up to me and smacked the shit out of me. I was dazed for a minute and then I realized this bitch really hit me, then I had to fuck her up," Irie said.

That's the day Irie and I became best friends. Although Irie and me laugh about it, those girls haven't messed with her again. I'm so glad this is our senior year; we don't have to see them anymore once we graduate.

CHAPTER 1

THE LIT FOUR

ZAK

Three years later...

My sister and I are in our sophomore year of college and by then, we have learned the ends and outs of the campus. My sister has grown to enjoy smoking weed and knew the campus' hotspot. One day on our route to class she points her nose up like a dog marking its territory. She stops me in my tracks saying she smells weed. We walked a little further, noticing two females sitting outside, smoking before class.

"Where they get that weed from?" Q halted without hesitation to ask.

"Why? Yo! You smokin' or you five-o?" One responds.

"Who the fuck are you talking to? Do I look like five-o to you?" Q wanted to fuck her ass up but she wanted the weed more, so she didn't say anything else. She just stood there staring at them.

"Nah you good. Y'all can come smoke with us," she says, slyly extending the weed to us as she paid attention to our surroundings. "I definitely like you. I see you don't bite your tongue for shit."

"What's your name?"

"Qu-mar Davis, but everyone calls me Q."

"How y'all doin'? My name is Zakkiya Davis, everyone calls me Zak."

"Cool, cool...I'm Irie Clarke."

"Maria Moretti, but everyone calls me M."

"Are you two related? 'Cause y'all look just alike," Irie insinuates.

"Yes, this is my younger sister," I explain.

"Are you a freshman?" Maria asked.

"No. We're both sophomores," I answer.

Maria and Irie glared at each confused.

"Duh, we have the same father," Q said.

They all busted out laughing and continue to converse and smoke and gets to know one another. They hurried so they wouldn't be late for class, but before they went their separate ways, Irie told us about a party off campus grounds the following night. Q and I said we were down to go. They decide to meet in M's dorm room the next night so we could follow them to the party.

"Yo! This party is lit! Oh shit, let's go! The DJ is playing my song, *Fever*. Irie sings along as they hurried to the dance floor. "Tick Tock, Tick Tock, Bruck It Set, Bruck It Set It."

"Do that shit Irie! Girl you can dance your ass off. You gotta show me how to do that dance so I can whine on these mofo's," Q shouts over the music.

"I got you girl."

The girls were winding their hips to the beat of the music bouncing off the walls, without a care in the world. The innocence of the moment prevails as they only think of moving their bodies to the beat of the song and having a good time.

"Okay we can sit down now. I'm tired as hell trying to keep up with yo' ass," Q laughs as she tries to catch her breath.

"I don't know where they got this weed from, but it got me high as hell," Irie admits.

"I know one thing, if yo' ass don't pass that shit I'm fucking you up!"

"Here bitch, and y'all better not smoke it all. Ha! Ha!" Irie laughs out as she hands it over.

"No yo' ass better sip on some of that Ciroc, 'cause you ain't getting no more of this...now ha-ha that!" Q jokes.

"Y'all bitches goin' to class in the morning?" I question.

"Hell no! This party ain't over 'til 3 and you think I'm gonna be in class by 7. That professor can kiss my black ass," Irie exclaims.

"Irie your black ass is big as hell! I guess he got a lot of kissing to do," Q jokes.

"Y'all know I'm going to class because I'm not fucking up my 4.0 GPA. As a matter of fact, I'm out. Sis, I'll see you in the room. Deuces bitches!" I leave.

"Yea I'm out too. Q, you and Irie can stay here 'til it's over. Me and Zak, we out," M added.

The next morning Q was still stretched out in the bed while I was getting ready for class. I tried to get her up anyway because she knows she can't fuck up her basketball scholarship. This bitch ain't budging. She's so motionless I had to check to make sure she's breathing. I place my compact mirror close to her mouth to see if it fogs up. Thank God it does and since she was breathing, I leave to go to class.

M said Irie was out cold and she didn't even try to wake that crazy ass Jamaican up. M and I meet up in front of the dorm and walk to class together. We finish by 12:45pm and get something to eat. I didn't even leave the campus yet before my sister starts blowing up my phone asking me to bring her something to eat. This is our sophomore year in college and I noticed since meeting M and Irie she's been slipping. That's my blood so I'm not going let her slip too far. My daddy will kill me if I did.

Living with both of my parents was great, but my father cheated on Mom and I now have a sister, Q (Qu-mar Davis) who is only 6 months younger than me. That doesn't stop my father from thinking I'm supposed to watch her every move.

I love my sister. Even though my father is what some women would call a lying, cheating-ass-bastard who stepped out on my mother, got his sidepiece pregnant and had my sister, which brings absolutely no resentment to our relationship. We are close as hell and there's no bitch or dude that can ever come between us. Even though we have different mothers, my daddy made sure we were always around each other.

My mom took a lot of his shit because my sister was at our house all the time. She knew my dad was out there cheating but never said anything. She just continued to do what she did, and that is, be a good wife. I'm not sure if I could have accepted my husband bringing another child into our home. If she hadn't, I wouldn't have the relationship with my sister that we have now. Let alone a relationship at all. We never saw anything negative about Daddy or even saw any of his friends. Daddy kept my mom, Q, and I sheltered from his street life. No one even knew daddy was married with kids.

Q's mom was our father's hood chick. My mom was the good wife, with good credit and a good job. He didn't let my mother know too much of his street business. All she needed to know was that he was an engineer for the bus company. She always thought he sold drugs but never questioned him about it...she just knew.

Q's mom, Beatrice Jones or Ms. B., knew him for his street life. She said that's what attracted her to him. His swag. As Q and I got a little older we also thought our daddy was into more than just being an engineer, but we kept that between the two of us. Just like we knew Ms. B was helping him stash his drugs, his money, and bagging his drugs for him at her house. That's why he always had Q at our house.

When we were 12, my father moved us to Bloomsburg, Pennsylvania and brought Q with us. Three years later, at the age of 15, Ms. B. moved to the same town we lived in. My parents never talked to us about our sudden move, only that our last name will become Monroe from this point forward. But we didn't care after we saw the house we moved in to. Even though we relocated to another state, my father seems very paranoid for some reason and barely left the house. My Mom is a registered nurse and started working at the hospital in town about 6 months later. For one year my father didn't work, and only took us to and from school every day.

Q and I went to the same high school. She got a four-year basketball scholarship and daddy paid for me to go to college. He always made sure me and Q stayed in the latest shit. We were the baddest and the prettiest looking bitches in the school. Half of the school hated us, and the other half admired us. The haters knew—we may be pretty and know how to dress, but the heels will come off and we will whoop ass. We were unstoppable. They knew not to fuck with the Monroe sisters.

Q was with the point guard on the boys' basketball team and I dated the quarterback from the football team. Both of our dudes were well known and respected, so you know we got much respect from all the other guys, even though they wanted to get with us. They knew not to cross the line.

After high school everyone went their separate ways and here we are now at the end of our sophomore year in college. Our father still spoiled us as if we were little girls. He always sent money whenever we asked, only to go shopping with it. We made it through our sophomore year of college without Q getting kicked out for not showing up for class. We both are smart, so she aced all her finals as if she was there the whole time.

During the summer break we went home to chill with our parents. We knew our summer break would go by quick, so we had to catch up on family outings, shopping, and the men. I hung out with my mom a lot. She was asking how college was and if I was keeping up my GPA. We went to the spa, did some shopping, and sat down to nice dinners. I was close with both of my parents. I get my intelligence and finesse from my mom, while I got the heart of a lion, street smarts, and wisdom from my daddy.

Q is exactly like Daddy. He played basketball; she has his height, with his street smarts and wild side. Everyone thinks Q and I are twins because we look so much alike, with the only difference being Q's lighter skin. During the summer, Q chilled out with her mom for most of the summer so she could catch up on things with her. We found time for shopping and even met up with Irie and M.

M's government name is Maria Moretti - an Italian chick that's straight psycho, but you would never guess it by looking at her. M is very pretty with jet-black hair that stops at the crack of her ass, she has a body to die for and she's the quietest of the four of us.

The four of us together is crucial to anyone getting in our way. I'm laid back and observant but quick with my hands. Q is very quick tempered and doesn't think before she reacts. Irie is the one that will cut you so fast you won't even know until you saw the blood gushing out. M will kill you in the blink of an eye and have no conscience.

One day M recalled a story when her dad, who is a big-time mob boss, had a meeting at his house and she eavesdropped. Her dad was yelling at the guy because he didn't carry out a hit her dad put out on someone. When her dad noticed she was listening by the door, he called her in the room and told her if she ever wanted to be a boss, she has to handle situations like this. At the time she was only 13 and didn't know what kind of situation it was, but she knew that whatever her daddy said goes. The man was kneeling on thick plastic placed in the center of a circle surrounded by her father's friends.

"You want to be a boss," her father asked placing the gun in her hand.

"Yes," thirteen-year-old M responded.

"Shoot him in the head," her father demands.

She already knew how to shoot a gun because her father took her to the shooting range all the time.

"Suck it up bosses don't cry they shoot", her father said after noticing a single tear fall from her eye.

So she shot the guy in the head.

That's when we found out why M never shed a tear and acts like nothing fazes her. She said she didn't even have nightmares afterwards. She has an older sister Gabriella Moretti, "Gabbie", but her dad says she's not the boss type. He says M is just like him and because he doesn't have a son, he will train M as if she was his son—not his daughter. M loves her Dad to death and he will do anything for her. During our summer break she told us to come chill at her house, because her father was throwing a pool party for her. Of course, we responded "Just say when!" and went shopping for bathing suits.

Personally, I'm a Gucci Queen so I had on Gucci from head to toe. My shades, two-piece bathing suit, my shoes and bag were all Gucci. Q is a Chanel girl and rocks Chanel hard, looking like a super model on the runway. Irie was dressed in Dolce and Gabbana from head to toe and she was looking real cute. When we got to M's house she had on a two-piece Burberry bathing suit rocking some shades and a big hat like Mary J. Blige.

Once we saw her large embellished house, we were all amazed. "Oh shit, that's how this bitch is living?" Hell, I thought my dad had it going on until I saw how M's family was living. They had an eight-bedroom house with five bathrooms and a pool house.

Her family seems really nice. They told us to make ourselves at home and enjoy. We certainly did! They had so much food and liquor, but we had to go in M's room to smoke because her dad said smoking makes you lose your train of thought and M needs to be on point at all times. Just in case someone tries to rob her or a fight breaks out, she needs to be focused. I guess that's why M doesn't get too fucked up. If anything pops off, M has to stay ready. I'm about to take that advice and do the same because I don't want anyone to catch me slipping. Q loves her weed and refuses to fall back. When we go to the club, she won't smoke as much, because if she thinks someone has one up on her she will lose it. As for Irie, she claims she can't function without her weed.

After we finished smoking, we clean up and head back downstairs. M introduced us to her mom and sister before she took us over to her father. Shockingly, her dad looked good as hell. I pictured him as some big fat short roly-poly looking dude. He was the total opposite. He was tall, about 6'3 and muscular with jet-black hair and a mocha complexion. He looked so delectable I think I came on myself. You know I played it off like he was a regular dude. Unlike Irie...she was all giddy like a schoolgirl smiling hard and shit. She didn't even want to let his hand go when he shook it.

Q smacked her hand down and said, "Bitch, chill out! That's M's father!"

Irie was like, "Oh well. I guess I'm gonna be M's step mom!"

The whole time Irie was trying to give him googly eyes, he was staring at me. I played that shit off so cool. I simply said, "Nice meeting you" and walked off.

My sister knows me so well, she walked up behind me, "Bitch you think you're slick, you know what it is. That man is sweating you and you are sweating him. He might not be able to tell, but I'm your sister and I know your ass."

"Shut up! We will talk about this shit at home. You never know who is listening. You got that sis."

After that, we started mingling, dancing and getting our drink on. The party was so much fun and a lot of people were there. Her dad kept coming over, asking if I wanted anything and checking to see if I was okay. Irie's ass was feeling some kind of way, because he wasn't asking her shit.

"C'mere Zak," Q snaps. "I was peeping that bitch out because she kept cutting her eyes at you. Me and Irie are cool, but I will really hurt that bitch if she comes for you." She gives a snarky glare at Irie. "You know I can hold my own right?"

"I'm not worried about Irie at all," I agree.

As we were about to leave, her dad came over to us and said he hopes we'll come back to hang out before we go back to school. Irie was the first to say, "Of course we will." The only thing I said was, "The party was really nice and you have a lovely home. Goodnight."

You can tell by the look on his face that he was expecting more from me, but I gave him absolutely nothing. Irie leaned in for a hug and Mr. Moretti Jr. held his hand out to shake hers and said goodnight. I said my goodbyes and M walked us out. I'm not sure if M noticed or not, but she's not stupid. Eventually she'll start to wonder.

The ride home was very quiet. Irie was in the back not saying anything and I was deep in thought—about you know who—here goes Q wanting to start some shit.

"Yo, their house was nice as hell, right? M's father looks good!" All she needed to do was say something about Mr. Moretti Jr., and Irie was all in.

"Yeah I can see myself fucking him real good. Riding the shit out of him, cowgirl style," Irie stakes her claim.

I remain stoic.

"For real Irie? You would really fuck M's father?" Q asks.

"Just as sure as my name is Irie Clarke."

"Not for nothin', he wasn't even checkin' for you yo. Not that you're ugly or anything, but maybe you're just not his type. Never throw yourself on a dude and remember, he's M's father," Q admitted.

"You don't give a fuck about him being M's father. You're

only worrying about your sister. I saw how she was looking at him!" Irie scorned.

"Bitch! What the fuck you bringing me up for? For one you ain't see me do shit, 'cause I wasn't paying his ass no attention. And for the record, since you think you saw me looking at him, was he looking at you? Umm I'm waiting...exactly!" I interject.

Q began to laugh so hard, tears rolled down her cheeks.

"Irie, how the fuck you tryna come for Zak? You just mad 'cause that man wasn't paying yo' ass no attention. He was trying to get Zak's attention. Yo, we are all cool as hell. Don't let that shit fuck up a friendship. You know I'll fuck you up over my sister," Q says.

"Calm down Q, I don't want any problems with you and I don't want that man. I was just joking around. You know how I do. I'm just trying to get in where I fit in," Irie calms down.

Soon after, we dropped Irie at her home and said our good-byes. We drove silently maybe a block before we both burst into laughter.

"You know that bitch was mad as hell and you know she might tell M," Q says as she tries to catch her breath.

"No she won't 'cause that means she'll have to tell on herself," I remind her.

"Okay you got a point there. Watch her 'cause we all know how she gets down when she like a dude and someone is in her way. Do you remember when she mixed feces in the oxtail gravy, and gave it to that girl she found out was sleeping with her dude? When we get back to school, I don't care how many meals she cooks, don't eat or drink nothing from that crazy chick."

"Oh, best believe I'm not a fool! You know we were raised better than to eat from everybody anyway," I agree.

CHAPTER 2

SHIT, I'D FUCK HIM

ZAK

We stayed the night at our parent's house. We were still a little hyped from the party, so we stayed up most of the night reminiscing on old times.

"Q, do you remember the time we took daddy's car and met up with our boyfriends from high school?" I asked.

"Yes. I definitely remember that."

"As soon as we got out of the car to walk on his front porch, Daddy pulled up in my mom's car. He didn't even let us drive the car back home. He had the tow truck company tow it back." I tried to explain through my laughter.

"That shit was scary and funny at the same time. We were on punishment for two months because of that."

Although we questioned him many times wondering how he knew where to find us, it wasn't until later that we found out he had trackers on our cell phones.

My mind is all over the place right now, I've never slept with a married man before and not only is he married but he's my friend's father. Nah, I can't do M like that, that's my girl.

"Earth to Zak! Damn you must really be thinkin' hard about sleeping with Moretti Jr. Would you really fuck M's father?" Q giggles knowing exactly how to push my buttons.

"You know that's not my style, but damn Q! He looks good as hell and if he keeps pushing up on me, I don't know how long I'm going to push away."

"Well it's wrong...and I'm your sister so I can tell you that. If you decide to fuck him, I'm on your side no matter what. You know you'll have all those bitches coming for you— M, her Mom and Irie!" Q laughs so hard forgetting what time it is.

"Yea I know Q. I didn't say I plan on doing anything, but if it happens, shit...it just happens."

"Okay sis'. Just letting you know it's going to be some serious repercussions behind it if you do Zak." I shrug my shoulders like oh well. Q throws a pillow at me and we laugh hard then say goodnight.

The following weekend, M said her parents invited us to a dinner party at her house. I didn't want to say no because I don't want her to become suspicious of me becoming distant. Turning down the invite would make her suspicious because she knows we love to have a good time.

Although I won't have sex with Moretti Jr., I still have the urge to show him what I'm working with. So, I pulled out this really gorgeous black Gucci cocktail dress, with my black & red Gucci pumps and matching bag. My dress is simple but very elegant and most importantly, it fits every curve god blessed me with. Q slayed in a black Chanel dress with silver shoes and she looks very pretty. Irie texts Q to say she'll be driving herself to M's house. When Q read the text to me we just bust out laughing—nothing needed to be said. Instead we did a glamour check on one another before agreeing that we look perfect. We had to quickly say goodnight to our parents before scurrying to get on the road for the two and a half hour trek to M's. She mentioned her dad was going all out for this dinner, hiring a chef, servers, parking attendants...everything! Let Q tell it, he was doing all of this for me. Little does she know, I put this outfit on for him to sweat me. We were running late, but M texted Q to say her father will wait for all guests to start dinner.

"Bullshit! He's making everybody wait just for your ass. Their stomachs are probably growling and everything. He don't give a hell about them!" Q laughs at her own joke.

"Yo shut up Q! You are so stupid."

"Maybe. But you know I'm telling the truth."

We finally arrived fifteen minutes late. Thank God we didn't have to search for a parking space, Mr. Moretti Jr. had valet parking. When the butler opens the door, Mr. Moretti Jr. stood in the foyer and welcomed us into his home. Moretti Jr. wore all black with a dinner jacket and black leather Italian shoes. M was right beside her dad to greet us. She was smiling from ear-to-ear happy we made it. I apologized for the tardiness, blaming it on heavy traffic. Mr. Moretti Jr. offered that there was no need to explain, he had no intentions of starting this dinner party without me. The room seemed to become extremely quiet, so he cleaned it up by saying, my wife and I like for all guests to be in attendance before we eat. Q cut her eyes at me and I just smiled.

Dinner was excellent. We were served bruschetta, stuffed mushrooms, and fried calamari for appetizers. For the main course it was lasagna, chicken parmesan, vegetables, and bread. Cannolis and tiramisu for dessert. As we ate, everyone was talking about family. Mrs. Moretti took this opportunity to ask about our parents; specifically their names and what they do for a living.

I can't disclose everything. There are some things no one should know about the Davis family. My father never allowed us to bring friends to our home, nor did daddy. I can't mention our impromptu dead-of-night escape and name change. So, no one even knows our last name is actually Davis. It's one of many family secrets. My parent's names are Steven and Sue

Monroe. Sue is my mom's middle name, but Lord only knows where my dad got the name Steven. So, I told her the only thing I could—my mom is a nurse and daddy is an engineer for transit, which is technically half the truth.

Q and I have been telling this same story for seven years now and it's starting to seem real. It honestly makes me feel as though I don't know who I am. I made a mental note to have a serious conversation with my parents about all of this, because they keep putting us off saying when the time is right, we'll talk. We are in college and they still treat us like little girls. It's a must that we know what the family's secret is.

We had a great time with the Moretti family. However, there's something really strange about her sister Gabbie, who looks as if she's off in space somewhere. She's very pretty and looks a lot like M with her long jet-black hair, but she doesn't talk to her family much at all. The only time she engaged in conversation was with Q, Irie and me. I also noticed that she didn't eat, just nibbled over her food. I'm not quite sure what it is, but I'll be sure to bring her up to M later.

"Did you all enjoy the dinner?" Mrs. Moretti asked.

"Yes, dinner was delicious and I'm stuffed," the girls say in almost unison.

Mr. Moretti Jr. was polite tonight, he wasn't giving me those same googly eyes like last time too much, but he blew me a kiss. I ignored it, refusing to even smile his way.

As the night wounds down, we offered to help clear the table, but he gloats about having people who handle that. Instead, he implores us to make ourselves comfortable.

All dinner guests went into the family room to sit and talk. However, that's not really something Q and me wanted to do with them. We are not used to sharing our family business with anyone—Mrs. Moretti seems to want to know way too much info for my liking. Her shady guise is making me think she has ulterior motives, and she's getting on my last damn nerves with all these questions. I hope she doesn't think I'm naïve just because I'm young. The only information she will get out of me is what I've already given her and that's the same info everyone gets—no more no less. M and Irie don't even know where we live. Since Mrs. Moretti wants to ask questions, I began to ask my own, starting with Gabbie.

"Gabbie, do you have a steady boyfriend? Planning to get married soon?" I asked averting the attention quickly away from my sister and I. Unfortunately for me, from the look on their faces, that wasn't a good question to start with.

Her eyes got watery and she glared at Maria with hatred in her eyes. M didn't say a word and tried to keep her cool, but I can tell something was seriously wrong between the two of them. Maybe M's sneaky self slept with her older sister's man.

Mrs. Moretti told Gabbie to get up and excuse herself in a very harsh, clinched-teeth manner.

"I apologize. I didn't mean to upset her," I admitted.

"It's fine hun. You had no way of knowing that the man she loved and was going to marry, left her. He changed his number and never returned."

I immediately felt my stomach sink to the floor as the revelation saddened me. I felt so bad for Gabbie and sincerely apologized, but I can tell they were not telling the truth. However, I went along with it, making a mental note to become cool with Gabbie so I can find out the Moretti's secret. She's the perfect person to get all the dirt from. It's obvious.

At that point I knew it was time to go home. We all said goodnight and waited outside for our cars. Once there, Irie obviously seemed as if she were pressed to say something to me. She hadn't said two words to me all night and now this bitch got words.

"Oh my God Zak! What was that all about? Gabbie almost had a nervous breakdown. I'm glad her mother told her to excuse herself. Did you see how she looked at M?" Irie exclaimed.

I'm not telling this hating ass bitch what I really think. "She must have really loved him, poor thing." Just then our cars arrived. "Okay girl. Goodnight."

She got in her car, as Q and me got into my car.

"Oh shit! What the hell is going on in that house? Did you see how she looked at M? Those two bitches are beefing hard. She looked at her like she wanted to kill her ass. Mrs. Moretti seemed to get nervous, but M & Mr. Moretti Jr. played that shit off smooth as hell," Q word vomited.

"You know I pay attention to everything. M was shocked – she probably wasn't expecting me to ask her sister anything. My question just came out of left field and she didn't have time to prepare a poker face. I only asked because she's still at home with her parents and when they give parties, she's there by herself, never with a date. She seems as though she doesn't fit in that family, and after tonight, it's as if she doesn't even like their asses.

"Oh sis', you know we have to get to the bottom of this, 'cause my nosy ass wants to know what the fuck is going on," Q said.

"Yes, we will get to the bottom of it all right. I made a mental note to get close to Gabbie, 'cause I think she will tell it all. If we mention that ex-boyfriend of hers, she'll open up. M is going to be extra careful now with her sister being around us, so we won't even bring up what happened tonight."

Q just bursts into laughter.

"Yo! What the hell are you laughing for now, silly?"

"We're sitting up here tryin' to figure out the Moretti's family secret, when clearly we have a big one in the Davis family. We can't even use our real last name!" She laughs aloud again, "and not to mention our impromptu move in the middle of the night. What the hell was that all about anyway? Every time we ask our parents about it, they keep telling us we'll talk about it later."

"You have a point sis', 'cause I wanna know bad as hell. But like you said they keep putting us off. No matter how many times we ask, they are not going to tell us until they're ready," I add.

CHAPTER 3

WE RUN VIRGINIA
ZAK

Before the summer was over, we went to visit our grandparents down in Alexandria, Virginia for two weeks without our parents. The last time we saw our grandparents was at our high school graduation. Needless to say, we were all due for a visit, we missed them dearly. When we pulled up to the house the entire family was outside waiting. My grandparents, Auntie Jackie and all ten of our cousins were outside for our arrival.

The house is enormous, with seven bedrooms, a finished basement and attic, and a one-bedroom guesthouse in the back. We hadn't seen our cousins since we were younger, but we kept in touch through text and social media. My male cousins grabbed our luggage from the car and carried them in for us as the rest of the family hauled us into the house.

Everyone was so excited to see us and we felt the same. Thank goodness my Grandmother cooked a feast because we were starving. Our southern manners made us clean ourselves up first before we can delve into all this great food. We couldn't wait to catch up with everyone, talk about old times and what's new in everyone's lives. It wasn't long before we were playing games and making cocktails.

For the first time Q and I are around family. That was the moment I realized we missed out on so much. They made plans for us for the entire time we were there so we wouldn't be bored. They had an entire itinerary in place for us. One day the amusement parks, another, a huge cookout along with swimming in the pool. They also had a day planned for shopping and just hanging around the enormous house my dad bought for his parents years ago.

We were tired from the long drive. After staying up a little while longer talking, we all got ready to turn in for the night. Q and I shared a room, which worked for us because we had things to discuss. As soon as we got inside our bedroom we begin conversing.

"Where in the hell all these cousins come from? I thought daddy only had one sister. Damn she was a whore...and the twins are definitely mixed. Their hair is jet black and trinity's hair is down her back," I said.

Q laughs out, "and you call me stupid? You can tell we are all related because we all look alike. But yes, you can definitely tell the twins are mixed. Some of the other cousin looked mixed too. Seems it's more secrets in the Davis family than just our household. We need to see what we can find out while we are here since our parents won't tell us anything."

"You are my sister for real cause I was thinking the same thing," I acknowledged. "Goodnight."

The next morning during breakfast, I didn't hesitate to bring up a conversation about the cousins.

"Are they all your kids?" I asked Aunt Jackie. She was so shocked by my out-of-the-blue question that she almost choked on her iced tea.

"Oh no, I have three kids; Chelsea, Camron & Kyle and the rest are spread out between your uncles," she responds grabbing a napkin from the table to wipe her mouth.

"We have uncles?" Q and I blurt out simultaneously.

"We only knew of you Aunt Jackie. How many Uncles do we have?" I ask.

"I have—well I had three brothers, of course one is your dad," Aunt Jackie responds.

"So where are my two uncles? Are they coming so we can meet them?" Q asked.

Our cousins Trent and Jamar enter the room to join the conversation.

"No 'lil cuz, my dad won't be coming. He was killed when I was young. You know the twins Tristan and Trinity are my baby brother and sister," Trent says.

"Well, my dad ain't comin' to see nobody. He never came back to see us either, so don't feel bad. He left the four of us behind – me, Jamil, Destiny & Machi. (Jamar says angrily?) *Jamar displays an angry look on his face while telling us about their dad.*

"He dropped off the face of the earth and never returned. So, we have a deadbeat dad." *He threw his hands in the air while shaking his head in disgust.* "That's why we all live here with Grandma and Granddaddy. Your dad bought this house for our Grandparents, 'cause they had to care for all of us. The truth is, they use to live in a much smaller house," Jamar informs us.

"What I can't understand is why my Dad never mentioned the fact that he had two brothers?" Q wonders.

I noticed my grandmother never said a word. My Granddaddy was in the den watching television, so he didn't know what we were talking about anyway. I watch my Grandmother get up and walk into the kitchen. When Q said she couldn't understand why my father never mentioned his brothers, my Grams couldn't take any more, which was clear by the sad expression on her face. My Aunt Jackie went into the kitchen after her. I'm quite sure she went to console her. I thought it was time to end that conversation because it was upsetting her too much. Q and I weren't expecting to find out any of this family history. We wanted to know more but not at my Grams expense. We'll just have to continue this conversation with our father.

"Okay, let's talk about something more uplifting, 'cause we are getting Grams upset," I say.

"I will come to your room later, I have something to tell you," my cousin Destiny said as she sits beside me. I just gave her a head nod and winked.

Later that night when we all went to bed, Destiny came to our room and of course, Q's nosey ass was ready.

Destiny enters our room and closes the door, then began to pace the room. Q & I sat up in our beds with anticipation. "I'm going to get straight to the point. When Q said she can't understand why your father never mentioned the fact that he had two brothers, I noticed Grams getting upset. I remember years ago your dad came to the house in the middle of the night and was talking to our grandparents." Destiny paused as if she were remembering it like it was yesterday. "He seemed out of breath, tired and looked crazy." She motioned her hands around her head to gesture a crazed look. "He gave Granddaddy a duffle bag full of money and told him something about my father and Uncle Phil. I couldn't hear what he was saying, but I remember Grams started screaming and crying. She smacked your Dad in the face and walked off. Granddaddy was very calm and took your daddy and walked into another room. I went back upstairs. I tried to tell Jamar & Jamil but they wouldn't wake up, so I just got back in the bed wondering what that was all about." Destiny stopped pacing the room and sat beside me on the bed. Her voice drifted off into sadness.

All Q and I could do was look blankly at one another in awe before averting our attention back to her. There were no words we could come up with because we had absolutely no clue what the hell she was talking about. That fact alone was beginning to make my blood boil. Why do our parents insist on keeping us in the dark like this when clearly the rest of the family knows everything.

"The next day Grams was so upset, she wouldn't come out of her room, so Granddaddy had to break the news to Trent that his Daddy was killed the night before. At that time, we didn't know my Dad would never come back to get us, but he never did. My Dad didn't even show up for Uncle Phil's funeral.

"That's some deep shit not to show up for his brother's funeral," Q said while shaking her head.

"Right after that we got a bunch of phone calls, but the caller never said anything. Grams would just hold the phone to her ear and cry. Granddaddy used to say, that ain't nobody but James checking in," Destiny continues.

"Yeah, that probably was your dad. He was missing y'all, just like y'all were missing him," I added.

"I guess so," Destiny responded somberly.

When your father told Granddaddy, he bought this house for them, Grams refused to move in at first. First, she said she didn't want anything from your Dad. Second, my Dad wouldn't be able to contact her, 'cause she knew in her heart that it was him on the other end of the mysterious phone calls," she says staring at the floor.

I had a look of confusion and concern, immediately thinking my father had his brother killed for some reason. My heart started beating extremely fast and my emotions were all over the place. No wonder my Daddy didn't tell us he had brothers. How could he tell us if he had one of them killed or killed him himself?

Destiny startled me out of my deep thoughts.

"I hope I didn't scare y'all but there's so many secrets in this family. It's scary. We never found out what happened to Uncle Phil and we still don't know where our Dad is. We think your Dad knows the truth."

"No, you didn't scare us at all. We were actually hoping we

could get some information from Grams and Granddaddy, but I don't think we would have gotten this much," I assure her. I tried exuding confidence in that fact, but the truth is, I'm not sure.

"Okay wait. I want you to go back to the night my Dad came to give Granddaddy the bag full of money. How was Granddaddy so calm when he just informed him that his son was killed?" Q questions.

"I don't know cousin. Everything I just told you is all I know. They never talk about it. Since you two have been here, this the first time my Dad, your Dad and Uncle Phil has been mentioned in years. They act as if nothing ever happened and their three sons never existed," Destiny responds.

"Well you also said when Granddaddy told y'all about Uncle Phil getting killed, you said he only told Trent. Why didn't he tell the twins?" Q asks.

"Oh yeah, the twins weren't born then. Uncle Phil's fiancé was eight months pregnant. When she had the twins, Grandma and Granddaddy raised them...with the help of Aunt Jackie of course.

"Why couldn't she raise the twins herself?" Q interjects.

"I don't know, we all think she might've killed herself after Uncle Phil's death."

"Damn! That's some deep shit!" Q exclaims.

"What's up with Auntie Jackie? Does she hold secrets too? Hell! I just want to know if there's any adult in this family that we can talk to," I asked.

"Actually, Aunt Jackie is the one you can go to for any and everything. Every now and again we talk about it. Some things I don't think I want to know, but at times I do want to clear my conscience," Destiny says. "I'm not going to lie but for a long time I thought your Dad had something to do with Uncle Phil getting killed.

Oh my God! That's the same thing I was thinking. My Grams

probably thinks the same. That's why she didn't want to accept this house from him.

Not long after, Destiny went to her room, which gave Q and me the opportunity to discuss what she told us.

"I'm not sure if I wanna know another damn thing," I admit.

"Bullshit! This is some juicy shit and I'm here for all of it," Q blurts.

"Yo! You are nosey as hell, go to sleep...goodnight sis love you."

"Love you too sissy."

The next morning, I laid in bed thinking of everything Destiny told us. I couldn't discard this overwhelming feeling I have, but I don't want this to ruin our time here with the family either.

Q turned in the bed to face my bed with her hand resting on the side of her face.

"Zak, are you awake?"

"Yes, I'm awake Q."

"I don't know about you, but that shit Destiny told us last night had me fucked up. What if Daddy killed his brother?"

"Yeah, my exact same thought," I say shaking my head.

"Nope! Nope! I'm not going to think like this. Not our Daddy. He would never. When we get back home, we have to have this conversation with him."

"Yeah, sure, we're just going to say, "Daddy did you kill your brother? The brother that we don't even know about.""

"Well older sister, I'm leaving this up to you to figure out, but for now, we have to get up to shower and go downstairs with the rest of the family."

Once we get downstairs, we had our game face on. I'm ready to do something different, so I asked them if there were any clubs down here we could go to?

"Of course we do. One of my boys and his wifey owns one of

the clubs down here. They are trying to open a club up there in your hometown, too," Jamil says.

"All right then, we are going out tonight," Q replies.

We were rolling deep that night; all ten of us went to the club. Q and I didn't know how much respect our cousins got until we went out with them. They were like ghetto superstars, the male and the female cousins. Hell, I was glad to be with them, any other time bitches want to hang out with us. I felt like a groupie chilling with them. As we pulled up, we could hear the music from inside the club. It was a long line of people outside waiting to get in. The huge bouncer nodded to my cousin Jamar and we were ushered right inside without waiting, as if we were celebrities. They escorted us straight to the VIP section, and on queue, the waitresses brought bottles over to us.

First, we met his boy Kareem and his wife Iman, the club owners. They were so down to earth, and all drinks were free that night. For Q and me, that meant Long Islands all night.

"Damn! I didn't know Virginia had this many good-looking guys. I'm 'bout to relocate," I joke.

"Come on cuz, don't make me have to hurt one of these dudes in here. They saw y'all come in here with us so they won't violate. They will ask first, trust me.

"Sure enough, here come two guys. They went straight to Jamil and Jamar. We're not sure what was said, but they eventually came over to us to speak. They asked if we wanted to dance, but we never go for the first who come seek us out. You have to make them wait a bit. So, we told them maybe on the next song, so they politely smiled and walked away.

We're in VIP, drinking, dancing, and enjoying the night. Everybody down here seemed so cool. I just felt at home and announced I might have to come down every summer. Of course Iman welcomed the thought, saying any family of our cousins is family of hers. She even suggested she'd get our number from the cousins so that when they come up north to visit, she could chill out with us. An idea my sister and me couldn't wait to happen. We enjoyed the rest of the night until the club closed, then headed back to our grandparent's.

"So, did y'all enjoy the VA club life?" Jamil gloats.

"Oh yeah! It was lit. Too bad we have to go back so soon! Just know we will be back," Q says excited.

On our last night I want all of us to sit and talk as family. As planned, ten of us cousins were in the family room talking while our grandparents, Aunt Jackie and the twins went to bed.

"Okay, Q and I wanted us to have this talk because we don't really know anything about the family. We are tired of being left out of what's going on," I start.

"Well, cuz, since I'm the oldest I'm going to let you know what's up. I trust since you are Uncle Tony's daughter—my bad Uncle Steven," Trent clears his throat and laughs out, "you can keep a secret."

Q and I shake our heads agreeing that whatever is said, stays here.

Trent continues. "Well, myself, along with Machi, Jamar, Jamil, Cam and Kyle we run Virginia and it was passed down to us from grandpa and all of our dads. That's why when your father came to the house that night to tell Grandpa about our dad getting killed, he was so calm. It came with the lifestyle. I'm not saying he wasn't hurt because trust me he was devastated, but he couldn't show emotions. He was taught to handle all situations."

"Word! Let me find out, my Grandfather is gangster! This shit is crazy!" Q exclaims.

"It's real life for us down here. We try to keep a very low profile because that's how Pop likes it," Jamar adds.

"Did y'all have to put in any work?" I inquire.

"Did we? Just know they don't fuck with your cousins at all.

They know their body parts will be spread across the country," Jamil says.

"I'm glad to know we have cousins that's 'bout it. We can fight, but I don't know if I can kill someone. I do want to learn how to shoot a gun. I ain't no killa, but don't push me." Q smiles.

"Yo' cuddy, you funny as hell. You have our blood in you, so trust me it's only because you didn't have a reason to kill, but I'm quite sure you can do it.

I'm surprised Uncle Tony didn't teach y'all how to use a gun," Trent says.

"Well can't you tell...he didn't even tell us we had Uncles. You think he is going to teach us how to use a gun?" Q laughs.

"We taught Chelsea and Destiny how to fight, and how to use a gun. Bitches know not to step to them. We got y'all back if you ever get into any beef. No matter how big or small, we are just a phone call away," Trent reassures.

"You know I'm there. I love to fight...it's therapy for my soul!" Chelsea laughs out.

"Well, I know how to fight very well, but I don't have time for all that because bitches like to scratch you in the face. I'll just shoot a bitch and get it over with," Destiny adds.

"I'm glad to know y'all have our backs because it's just me and Q up there. We have two chicks that we're cool with. I guess if we got into anything, they would have our backs, but I don't trust either of them at all," I admit.

"Fuck both of those bitches! They don't have to have your back, we got y'all. If you have to think twice about a person, then something is not right. Don't chalk that shit up as if it was just a thought, that's a warning. Listen to it.

Yo', I'm coming up there once y'all get back to school and on y'all first break I'm there," Chelsea says.

"You mean we're there. You know how we do in this family. **One for all and all for one,**" Destiny interrupts.

"Even though the twins are young, they are actually the crazy ones. Please don't get Trinity started. For her to be so young, we can see the crazy all in her face. That chick is looney for real and Tristan is a different kind of crazy. He doesn't cry. Even if he gets a whooping he will not cry. We are definitely going to have our hands full with those two," Jamil adds shaking his head.

CHAPTER 4

GUCCI EVERYTHING

ZAK

It's finally time to head back to our life of secrets in Pennsylvania. Our larger than expected family helped load the car before somberly sharing their goodbyes. We promised that we would stay in touch and return to visit soon, and we definitely meant it. My sister and I had a great time getting to know them, but we are only leaving here with more questions than answers. We have to get our parents to spill the damn beans already. We're not little girls anymore and can handle the truth. Hell, we learned a shit load of stuff in just a few days and we're still standing.

The ride back was totally different from when we drove there. We know we have to ask our parents, especially our dad, these questions. We couldn't stop talking about it amongst ourselves.

"How are we going to ask Dad about his brothers? He has to know we'd find out while being down there," I said.

"You heard Aunt Jackie when we were leaving. She made it clear we need to discuss this with our father. She must be okay with us telling him she told us some things."

"So if he asks how we found out, you think we should pin it on our Aunt?" I ask.

"Well, I guess. Aunt Jackie don't seem to bite her tongue. I think she can handle Daddy."

"You know there isn't too many things that I'm afraid of, but I'm really nervous about this Q. So many things went through my mind last night and I couldn't sleep. What if Daddy had something to do with his own brother getting killed and the other one is missing in action? We know how stern Daddy can be, but I couldn't fathom the idea of him killing his own brother."

"Here you go with your corny ass," Q laughs out loud at my conspiracy theories. "I can believe Daddy is a killer, but I bet all the money I have that Daddy wouldn't and didn't kill his brother. We just have to get to the bottom of this with Daddy. So, we can stop assuming."

"Okay. Don't say anything when we get back. We can at least enjoy the last two weeks of being home before we drop a bomb on him."

"Whatever you say sis'. I'll be ready when you're ready," Q agrees.

Is there ever really a good time to accuse your father of murder?

As soon as we got to the house our parents drilled us with so many questions. I don't know if it's because they know we found out some of the family's secrets, but it seemed like my Dad was so concerned about what happened while we were in Virginia. Of course, we decided to stick to our plan and elude them, only relaying how much fun we had. We told them about the cookouts, amusement parks & the great food Grams cooked for us. Which is all true, so it wasn't like we were lying. We decided to get away from the questioning by way of being tired from the drive and going to bed.

"Oh, you girls are not going to eat anything first?" Mom asked.

"No Ma. Grams packed us plenty of food for the road. I'm

tired. Q didn't help me drive there or back, so I don't know why she's so tired, but goodnight. Love you guys."

I need to clear my mind before my dad could ask any more questions. I know I was the one who said let's just wait before we say anything, but I don't know how long that's going to last. So, Q and I made our way upstairs to discuss how long we may be able to keep up this charade. First, we called M. Then she called Irie on the three way like we used to back in the day, to let them know we're back.

"I'm so glad y'all are back, I missed you two," M admitted.

"I missed you bitches too. So, what's up? What are we doing?" Irie asked.

I gave my sister the *bullshit* face at Irie's comment. This chick is phony as hell.

"Well, we can hook up tomorrow 'cause I'm about to take it down," I offer.

"Cool. We'll meet here at my house tomorrow around 11am. We have to go shopping. School starts in two weeks," M said.

"Are we still getting the house? I'm asking, 'cause this will be me and M's last year, and I don't want to be on campus," Irie whined.

"Oh well, that was one of the things I had to tell you. My Dad already got a four-bedroom house for us and we don't have to worry about the bills. He said just do well in school, that's all he cares about," M said nonchalantly as if the news was just another day in the life of Maria.

"Word? That's what I'm talking about! Free room and board. Just let your pops know that Zak and I will have one more year after your ass graduates, so is he going to kick us out the house?" Q laughs but is dead serious.

"No crazy! He knows you two are a year under us. He said he loves you and not to worry. You can stay at the house for your last year."

"Tell your Dad I said we love him too and thanks!" Q smiles.

"See you tomorrow ladies," I said.

"Yo, that man loves your ass. He just made sure you have a house to live in for the remainder of your college years," Q mocked.

"Umm hello! His daughter will be there at least one of those years. So stop making it seem like whatever he does, he's doing it for me."

"Zak you don't have to put on a front for me. You know as well as I know, that house is for you. This is M's senior year and he just decided to get a house," she sucks her teeth and rolls her eyes. "Okay let's make a bet. Tomorrow we will bring up the house situation and ask M what made her get a house and it's her last year? I bet she says her dad thought of it."

I suck my teeth. "You get on my nerves, but okay, it's a bet."

The next day we got up early and my mom fixed us breakfast. I felt bad that I didn't eat last night, so Q and I made sure we ate the breakfast she prepared for us. While eating, I told Daddy that we were going back-to-school shopping and we needed money, so he quickly handed over his black card. We were shocked 'cause he never gave us the black card. We shoved the food in our mouths to get the hell out of there before he could change his mind. My mom looked at him like he was crazy. She just cleared the table and went into the kitchen.

Q and I were out the door. I told her she was the chauffeur for today. We get to M's house on time this morning. *I guess I need to let Q drive all the time.* When we walked in, Mrs. Moretti asked if we wanted anything for breakfast, we declined having already eaten. Mr. Moretti Jr. walked out of the kitchen and acted as if he was surprised to see us. He gave us both a hug and whispered in my ear that he had something for me, just as M came downstairs to inform us that we were waiting on Irie to leave then gets a text.

"Oh, she's pulling up now. We can wait outside," M says as she reaches us.

Mr. Moretti Jr. walked us outside, following behind me as he sneakily handed me an envelope with a card inside. I thought about graciously taking it, but I don't want him to get the wrong idea. I politely declined his gift, but he silently begged me to take it, so I did. I placed it inside my Gucci bag and turned away from him.

I didn't want to leave my car parked at M's house, only because my dad wants us to be extra cautious with our personal belongings. Our cars are registered under our dad's assumed name, Steven Monroe, with a make-believe business address. I explained to M that Q and I will drive in my car so we can just go home instead of coming back to her house. M wanted all of us to be in the same car, but she said she understands.

"Yes, we are going in Zak's car 'cause she got me chauffeuring her ass all day and I'm not driving all around town," Q jumps in.

I love my sister because she is always on point.

"Okay sis, what was I just agreeing to?" Q asks.

"Mr. Moretti Jr. whispered in my ear and said he had something for me and when we walked outside, he handed me this envelope."

"Well bitch, open it and see what's inside."

"Okay calm down." I open the plain white envelope and pulled the card out. Before I could open it, large bills slide out of it. "Oh shit! This card is filled with a bunch of hundred-dollar bills."

"Get the fuck out of here! How much is it?" She says excitedly, slowly veering from our driving lane.

"Bitch you better watch the road! If you kill us, we can't spend his money. No wonder this envelope was so heavy, it's thousands of dollars in here." *Clearly he's used to luring women in with his money.*

"Okay tell me the truth...did you already fuck him? 'Cause I want to know why he gave you that money?"

"What! No, I didn't Q. And you know you'd be the first to know! Damn, shut up let me read the card."

Hi Zak,

I don't want you to think I'm trying to buy your affection, because I'm not, but I really like you and it's not much I wouldn't do for you. I think you are a gorgeous young lady. I know this is an awkward situation, being you're my daughter's friend. I won't let this disrupt the friendship you two have, so this will be our secret. I have much more to offer you than what's in the card, but I didn't want to scare you away. If you will allow me to take care of you like a man's supposed to, you won't regret it, I promise. Once you get to the mall go into the Gucci store and give them your name and tell them you have an order there. Everything is already paid for, and yes, I pay attention to everything you wear.

If you decide to pick up the items, that will be your answer to us seeing each other. If you decide to leave the items, then I will understand. You can keep the money regardless of your answer. Just so we're clear, I'm not some old creep looking to get in your panties. There's something that draws me to you when I look in your eyes. I hope you allow me the pleasure of finding out just what that is.

"Wow, sis' what are you going to do?" Q takes one hand off the steering wheel while shaking it at me. "I told you Mr. Moretti Jr. was in love with you. You know you're stepping into a danger zone 'cause that man is serious about you. He is married and that is our friend's father." Q shakes her head. "What if you just want to test the waters to see how the sex is and then you don't want to be bothered anymore, but he's not ready to stop seeing you, then what?" Q tilts her head to the side. "I don't think this is a good idea, he gave you thousands and there's no telling what he bought you at the Gucci store. I don't like this at all but again, I got your back when those bitches come for you."

I just sit there quietly taking it all in. I don't know what I've gotten myself into. I shouldn't accept anything from him…he's freaking married. Maybe I'll just let him know this is a big mistake. It's not like I need anything from him.

We arrive at the mall and shop until we are so tired and completely drained. We stopped to get a bite to eat and for some reason, my curiosity got the better of me. "Fuck it, I'm going to the Gucci store," I blurt out.

Q of course knew what I meant, but this other bitch just had to make a comment.

"Yeah, Miss Gucci Queen. I was shocked that you just walked right pass the Gucci store and didn't go inside. What, are you on a budget?" Irie questioned.

"You know what Irie, I'm going to let you slide with that one 'cause you know better than that," I replied.

We headed over to the Gucci store and were immediately approached by a well-dressed, blonde sales associate.

"May I help you ladies," the blonde asked.

"Yes, my name is Zakkiya. I believe you have something waiting for me?" I ask.

"Oh yes! Miss Zakkiya! We were waiting on you. Please have a seat and make yourself comfortable. Would you like something to drink?"

"Sure, I'll have a glass of iced tea please," I request.

"Would your guest like anything?" The blonde gestures toward my sister.

"Oh, yes my dear, I'll have a glass of iced tea as well, thank you," she tries to emulate what she believes is a proper tone.

Irie stood there with a stunned hater look on her face, while M just said, "no thank you, we're fine."

For the first time I think M was jealous. She's used to all the attention being on her and everyone catering to her needs in stores. Little did she know, all of this is courtesy of her dear Daddy.

"So, Irie do you still think my sister is on a budget?" Q says with laughter behind her sarcasm.

"Shut the hell up Q! I was just joking with Zak," Irie exclaims.

"Bitch you wasn't joking. Your ass was serious as hell. You saying you were joking cause you see how we do our shit!"

Well how Mr. Moretti does it! I think as I crack the fuck up in my head.

The sales associate came back with our drinks and we all got quiet. The other associates start bringing out racks of clothes, shoes, boots and bags. I was thinking I had to choose a few of the items from the racks, but the sales associate made it clear to me that everything was mine.

"Miss Zakkiya, none of these items have yet to be displayed online or in the stores. You are the first to have them. If you like we can have everything delivered to your house," The blonde informed me.

Oh shit he had to spend a fortune on all of this.

No wonder they are sucking up to me. I felt like Julia Roberts in Pretty Women. I really had to put my thinking cap on, because if he purchased these items and if I give them my address, he can easily get my address from them.

"M, what's the address to the house at school? I don't want to have to pack all of this when we leave.

Q looked at me smiled.

"Oh yes, let me give it to all of you now," M replied.

"M what made you get a house now, anyway? This is your last year of college," Q asked sneakily no doubt thinking of our little wager.

"Well Daddy asked me what did I think about getting a house so I don't have to stay on campus. Of course, I was like yes! He said he will make sure its big enough for all of us," M said simply.

I asked the sales associate to bag a few items for me to take with me that day and told Q to get her a few as well. Obviously she won the bet so I have to do something. Once I got the address from M, I asked the blonde to send the rest to our new home.

"Sure. Is there anything else I can do for you? You're all done here considering everything has been paid in advance," The blonde announced.

M and Irie both eyed me curiously.

"No ma'am that will be all. I appreciate your help," I respond not paying attention to the double-glare.

"No, thank you Miss Zakkiya. Here's my card, give me a call if you need anything. We have your address and phone number, so we'll keep you posted on the new items to come and yes, I know, before they go on display."

CHAPTER 5

BLACK CARD

ZAK

Q and I drive home with a car full of shopping bags. I know Irie is mad as hell. That bitch is probably talking a lot of shit right now.

"I don't know if you noticed it or not, but M wasn't feeling that shit in the Gucci store. When the clerk said everything was paid for, I was rolling in my head.

She's just used to everybody sucking up to her when she walks in stores because of her daddy's money," Q said.

"Well we have something in common then, 'cause they were sucking up to me too because of her daddy's money," I laugh out loud unable to contain it.

"Ooh my sis, just said a good joke. This shit is going down in the history book."

"Shut the fuck up Q! You're not the only funny one in the family."

"Okay, you just blew it with that corny shit," she imitates me, *"you're not the only funny one in the family.* Who says that?"

The rest of the ride home was so quiet, I fell asleep. When Q woke me up, we were already in front of the house.

As soon as we brought all the bags in the house, dad's face dropped.

"Looks as if I have a large bill coming," he said.

"NAH. The mall had a huge sale this weekend," I eased.

My mom comes upstairs with us to look at the clothes we got from the mall. She has very good taste in clothes, so we always love to get her approval.

"So, I see you girls did very well with picking these outfits. What can I say...you learned from the best," Mom gloats. "I even see a few pieces I can borrow."

"Ma, please! Where are you going, that you'll need to borrow something like this?"

"Oh, don't sleep on your mother. I've been going out lately with some of my co-workers. We went out for dinner, drinks, and went to the comedy club last week."

"Oh, okay! My mother is finally coming out of her shell," I joked.

"I was never in a shell. I just played the roll of a good wife. But since you girls are grown and away at school and daddy is always working, let's just say it's my time to have fun now."

"Well excuse me, Miss Mother. You better do your thing," I snap my fingers like a proud daughter.

My Mom sashayed back down the stairs, but not before she grabbed three of our outfits. We just laughed as she closed the door.

Q and I were tired, but we didn't want to stay in the house. We called M, told her we wanted to go to the club tonight and she was down to go. I told her we would be at her house by 11— since the club doesn't start jumping until 12am anyway. Since we had a few hours to chill, I picked out what I was going to wear for later on and then I lay down. Before I could doze off to sleep, my thoughts took over. *I don't know if I really like him.* I am more infatuated about his looks. I didn't expect things to go this far. Zakkiya what have you gotten yourself into....

It felt as though I had just fallen asleep when my phone starts ringing. I didn't bother to look to see who was calling.

"Hello Zakkiya. Did you like your wardrobe?" The deep, sexy voice said on the other end. The sound of his voice jolts me up and I become completely excited... until I realize I never gave him my number.

"Mr. Moretti! How did you get my number?" I question.

"Well hello to you too, Miss Zakkiya."

"Hello Mr. Moretti, I'm just shocked to hear you on my phone. Now how did you get my number?"

"While Maria was sleeping I went through her phone and got your number, is that okay?"

Seriously? How does he not think that's crossing the line? His card said he wouldn't do anything to make M suspicious. He's already sneaking around to do some daredevil type shit. What the fuck! Although my initial response was anger, I quickly became a little turned on that he would do something like that for me. *God, I think there's something really wrong with me.*

"Well since you already have it, it's fine. All you had to do was ask me for it—and to answer your original question, yes, I loved the clothes and thank you." *Just keep it cool girl.*

"No need to thank me, I'm glad they were to your liking and anything for my Zakkiya."

His Zakkiya. Oh I don't do ownership well. "Oh, I'm yours now?"

"Yes, you are mine until you no longer want me, but I'm sure that won't happen."

"Well, I like that you have a lot of confidence in yourself, but you might want to come down off that cloud you're on a bit."

He chuckles. "Well yes of course I do. If I didn't, I wouldn't have pursued you," he responds choosing only to address part of my comment.

"You have a valid point. I can't wait to see what you plan to do with and for me."

"For you? Well, that's the easy part, with you? Hmmm...let's leave that to your imagination, but trust me, you'll enjoy it."

I have a feeling he may be right about that. "I hope you're ready to put in work Moretti Jr. You'll have to show me you can keep up."

He laughs. "She has jokes, I like that."

Before I know it, we've talked for far too long. Well, he did most of the talking because I was so turned on by his voice that I didn't want say anything sexual. Although he did mention how enthused he is with the thought of touching me in places that I didn't know could send me up the wall. The thought sends chills through my veins, making my clit twitch.

"Well, I'm not going to keep you from getting some rest, so I'll talk to you later. Oh, but before you hang up, I have something else for you."

"Okay...are you going to tell me or is it another one of your surprises?"

"No, it's not a surprise. I have a black card for you, so you can shop as you wish and pay for your books for school. I just have to think of a way to get it to you."

What! So many questions flood my mind, but mainly, how can he say he doesn't want to buy me in one breath, but then turn around and offer me a black card. Granted, I'm going to take and use the hell out of it...I just don't want to get caught out there because I decided to take a chance with some dude. For now, I need to make sure I come up with a way to get this card without giving him my address. A big fucking no-no.

"I'm sure a man of your caliber has another house your wife doesn't know about?"

"Actually, no Zakkiya I don't, but that's not a bad idea. I'll make sure to put that in my mental rolodex, but for now I don't. I do a lot of business at the Hilton hotel. I have a penthouse suite there. I will leave it at the front desk with your name on it, you can pick it up anytime tomorrow after 2:00pm."

"Sure, I can do that. Thank you, talk to you soon."

We both hang up and immediately my heart drops. Clearly, I'm in way too deep.

CHAPTER 6

BEEF

ZAK

I stayed up thinking of the conversation I just had with Moretti. His voice is smooth, deep, and seductive, which sent chills throughout my body. Everything about Moretti is sexy. Hearing his voice gave me unwavering feelings that I can't seem to shake.

I must have been in deep thought because Q was calling my name and I didn't even hear her.

"What in the hell got you daydreaming? I'm calling you and you didn't even hear me," Q said.

"Girl, while you were asleep Moretti called and we talked for at least an hour."

"Get the fuck out of here! How did he get your number? What did he say? Did he ask you to have sex with him? Where was he while he was talking to you? What if someone heard him say your name?" Obviously she's so excited she couldn't just choose one damn question.

"If you slow your ass down and let me finish, I'll tell you what we talked about." I slightly roll my eyes, but my sister knows me well enough to know I'm just joking around. "Now, as I was saying, he called to see if I liked the clothes he bought for me. When I asked him how he got my number? He told me he went through M's phone while she was sleeping to get it." I pause a moment and glare at my sister to await the reaction I know I'm about to get. "Then he tells me I was his."

"His! That sounds a bit possessive," she says as I raise my eyebrow at her. "Okay, okay go ahead finish. I'm just saying."

"He told me he had a black card for me, and he will leave it at the Hilton with the receptionist."

"Well, I'm all for the black card, but that comment about you being his. I really don't like that at all."

I stop talking and just stare at Q. Of course that comment is a red flag and I've already come to the conclusion that I want to see where this goes. I doubt there's a lot for me to lose in this situation considering he's the one married and going after one of his daughter's closest friends. As I'm deep in thought, Q sits quietly waiting for me to continue. Something she's never really good at, so Moretti seeing me as his possession must seriously have her concerned. I think maybe I should delve deeper into the conversation surrounding the comment.

"Q he asked if I liked the clothes and I said yes. When I thanked him, he said, 'No need to thank me, anything for my Zakkiya.' Then I asked him, 'Oh I'm yours now?' That's when he said, 'Yes. You're mine until you don't want me.'

So, to ease your conscience, he didn't necessarily say it in a possessive manner. You know I would have checked him."

"Oh, okay. I just don't want him thinking he has possession over you because he's buying Gucci clothes and giving black cards. He's not doing anything different than what you're already accustomed to."

"HE KNOWS THAT. That's why he's not coming with nothing less. Anyway, enough of that. Let's get ready so we can hit the club," I say starting to get up from the bed but she stops me.

"Wait. Answer this one question. Are you going to pick up the card?"

"What do you think?" I say with a devious grin on my face.

Q just smiles back at me knowing I'm no fool. We hop out of bed to get ready to for the club and the drive to M's house.

We get to M's house around 11:30 that night, but didn't go inside because we were running late. M and Irie came out and hopped in M's car and we headed to this new club M wanted us to try out. The club was packed. Once we got inside, we head for the VIP section as usual but for some reason the guard wouldn't let us in. M asked him what's good, we always sit in the VIP section every time we enter a club.

"Well things are a little different at this club. This section was bought out for this weekend. Invited guest only," the guard responded.

As soon as we were about to walk away from the guard at the entrance of the VIP section, Irie yells out.

"Yo! I know that bitch up there in the VIP section. Well actually, I know her man very well. He lives in Virginia. She doesn't like me because she thinks I'm chasing after her man."

"You got beef? What's good?" Q said, ready to defend her friend.

There were about fifteen or twenty people near the entrance of the VIP section and they stop dancing to look our way to see what was going on. They weren't discreet at all. One female pointed in our direction as she whispered something in her friend's ear. They are some nosy ass people ready to see what was about to pop off in the club.

"I know her dude from Virginia, but it's a long story between us. Anyway, she approached me and asked if I was fucking him?"

"We were about to fight, but of course everybody was pulling me back. You know I was ready to cut her ass." Irie explained as she pointed her finger up at the female sitting in VIP.

"Let me see her face so we know who we need to fuck up if shit pop off. Q says to Irie.

"Zak! Don't we know that chick right there from somewhere?" Q asked.

"That's who Irie is talking about?" I question.

"Yeah, that's her. Why, who is that? Her face does look familiar as hell though."

"Dummy, that's Iman from Virginia. They are like family to our family. We're not doing shit to her that's our peoples."

My sister needs to stop smoking. She doesn't remember shit.

"Irie, you better peace shit up with that one, because that's fam right there," I say.

"Why would you say I better peace shit up? She jumped in my face telling me what I better not do?" Irie begins to yell over the music at me.

The people in the VIP section and on the dance floor stopped to watch the commotion once again.

Irie was upset and her Jamaican accent started flowing. "Bombaclatt! Dis a sum fucked up shit."

"Well, you just said you were chillin' with her hus—," I try to get the words out but Irie cuts me off.

"For one it's not her husband and he was chillin' with me."

"Bitch! Don't cut me off while I'm talking, and that is her husband. If that's what he said and she said it is, then that's what it is. See that comment right there lets me know you were wrong. Why would you care whether he's her husband if you weren't trying to fuck him? Or were you trying to fuck him? Cause you are big mad right now, what's really good?"

My voice remains calm even though I'm mad as hell. I do not like scenes caused in public. That's just not my style. I walk away from Irie because everyone was staring. As soon as I walk away, I hear Irie's boost of confidence yell behind me.

"Oh, you tryna come for me Zak? I never really liked your ass any way. You swear you're all that and you're not, you ain't shit bitch!"

Before I could even turn back and get with that bitch, Q has already punched the shit out of her.

The stunned look on Irie's face makes even me feel guilty even though she deserved it. What's worst is the blow came from her bestie.

"Really Q? We are too close for that. Why would you do this shit in the fucking club? You didn't have to hit her," M said while she tries to help Irie.

"DON'T TELL me to fucking chill out M. That bitch is not going to stand here and talk slick to my sister and think it's okay," Q said while pointing her fingers at M.

"I told you before Q, I don't have beef with you. It's your sister I have a problem with," Irie tries to explain as M helps her to her feet.

Q laughs like a villain in some hero movie. "See that's where you're fucked up at. If you have a problem with her, you have a problem with me, no questions asked."

Irie stares at Q confused as if what she just said made absolutely no sense to her whatsoever. Clearly she's a fucking moron if she thinks Q would choose her over me.

As M takes Irie to the bathroom, of course all eyes were on us. During the commotion, Iman and Kareem noticed us. They came down next to us ready for war. Q and I went up in VIP and told them what happened.

"I know that chick you were just beefing with. Every time we come to Jersey she seems to run into Kareem," Iman says while giving Kareem a devilish stare.

"Yeah we know. That's how that beef started. She told us that she didn't like that bitch. At first, we didn't know who she was talking about. When we realized it was you, I told her she had to peace that shit up 'cause you're fam. She wasn't trying to hear what I had to say. She flipped on me and Q hooked off on her."

"Even though I tell Q all the time I can fight my own battles let me handle it."

Q shrugs her shoulders. "Oh well. I was standing right next to her, so I handled it. She acts like she doesn't want beef with me 'cause she knows how I get down. She needs to be scared of Zak, cause she's the crazy one. She's just more laid back, so Irie thinks Zak is a punk."

"She's about to find out what I'm made of," I add.

"We've only been open for one week and my own peoples have an altercation in our club." Iman says as they all shared a laugh.

"O shit! This y'all club?" Q asked with excitement. That's right I forgot you told us you were opening a club here in Jersey. I apologize. I don't want your club to have a bad rep because of me, because this shit is nice as hell.

"Thanks. No worries, everything is fine." Iman assured us.

For some reason Kareem was sitting in the corner not saying much and Iman kept giving him the evil eye.

We waited to see if M & Irie would come out of the bathroom, but I guess they must have gone home because we didn't see them for the rest of the night. M must really feel some kind of way about what Q did because she didn't text to tell us they were leaving or that they left.

"Fuck both of them bitches. If M starts acting shady because her and Irie are cool, then that bitch can get it too." Q was still amped and ready to fight.

I really don't like confrontation, but I don't let shit slide either. I may not start the bullshit, but I will finish it. I don't care if Q punched her. I'm still going to fuck her up. This bitch smiles in my face every day like we're cool and then have the audacity to say she never liked me anyway. That's some phony ass shit that I don't do. I guess she said how she truly feels. It's not over...

CHAPTER 7

FAKE & PHONY

ZAK

The next morning as I lay in bed, I was still in disbelief of what Irie said at the club. It's funny how someone can call you friend and then tell you they never liked you anyway. That's some fake ass shit. The ringing of my phone brought me out of my thoughts. Iman called before heading back to VA. She said she was checking on me and Q to make sure we were good.

"You know I have to let the fam know what happened," Iman says.

"Nah you don't have to tell them. Irie ain't crazy, she don't want any problems."

Iman contemplates silently for a moment, no doubt feeling as if she's keeping a secret from them. "Okay, I won't say anything this time, but you know if anything happens after that, the whole crew will be back up here."

"I'm sure they will and thanks for checking on us. By the way, your club is really nice. Make sure you call me when you come back to Jersey and we'll meet up with you." I say before ending the call with Iman.

After I hung up the phone with Iman, I hop in the shower

before getting dressed. When I get downstairs Q is about to head out the door to pick up her mom to have lunch.

While Q has family time with her mom, I went to the hotel to pick up the black card. I am nervous because I thought I was going to run into Moretti and he would want me to go upstairs with him. I know eventually that time will come, but I wasn't in the mood today because I still had thoughts about Irie's slick ass mouth. The ride to the hotel gave me time to reflect on everything Irie ever said to me, but I get a call from Q who tells me that she just ran into Irie and M.

"Where are you? Are you ok?" I yell.

"Those bitches don't want it. Irie tried to explain herself and she wants to apologize to you."

I suck my teeth at thought of that asshole apologizing.

"She explained that we all are about to move in together and she don't want the tension between us. She claims she smoked some weed before she left her house and it had her fucked up. She said her feelings were hurt when you didn't defend her."

"That bitch is full of shit. For one, Irie can handle her weed. She can't function without it. Now if she said she didn't get a chance to smoke I would have believed her. Tell her to miss me with that bullshit. That bitch said what she really feels when she said she never liked me and whatever else she said."

"I feel you on that, because she didn't even look sincere when she said it, but I guess she thinks we are boo-boo-the-fools. My Mom said both of them are not to be trusted. You know she's from the streets and can read a person very well."

"You know what, I'll play along with her fake ass apology, but I don't trust her. I really don't want to stay there with them, Q"

"It's up to you sis."

"I'll think about it, but tell your mom thanks for the heads up. We are definitely onto those bitches. We have to play the game right along with them."

"Okay me and Mom are here eating, you know I couldn't wait to tell you that. See you later."

"Alright, love you."

These bitches really think I'm a joke. Fuck both of them. I'm definitely fucking her father now. Best believe before those bitches graduate, I'm fucking Irie up. I don't let shit slide that easily. That's why I don't trust chicks now. They smile in your face and that shit is fake as hell. Fuck M too and her nosy ass mother. I know Irie is her friend, but I'll fuck M's ass up too. They got me fucked all the way up. I was rambling on and on because I was still upset about what happened at the club.

My mind was racing about those two bitches and I didn't realize I made it back home in record time.

When Q got back to the house my blood was still boiling, she thought something happened again. I told her nothing happened. I'm just thinking about what happened the other night.

"I'm gonna whoop Irie's ass and I'm going to make sure you're not around Q."

"Now why would you do that Zak?"

"Because Irie got me fucked up. She must think I can't handle my shit but trust I'm gonna get her."

"Okay you have a point. Come on, let's go downstairs so you can calm down." Q slightly pushes me to the door.

We went downstairs to watch TV, which my mom was already doing. We told her that we were coming to chill out with them. Mom gave us that suspicious look and said,

"I know you girls keep secrets among yourselves, but I can tell something is wrong. Whenever you girls are ready to talk, I'm here."

We just stared at her at first, confused that she knew something was up but smiled to avert her thoughts to press the issue.

Mom finally gets up to make us popcorn and we enjoyed the movie Taken together.

We only had three days left before we went back to school, so we spent that time with our parents. We stayed in the house watching movies, playing games, and just catching up. My mom asked what was going on with me because I seemed agitated about something. My mom and I are close, so I decided to tell her what happened at the club that night. All of it.

"Listen Zak, I don't know your friends at all, but you know females can be very jealous hearted for no reason at all. The comment she made, 'she never liked you anyway', she meant it. So you have to watch your back."

Q and I just sat beside her on the couch, listening to her every word as if she were a preacher and giving her Sunday morning sermon.

"I don't like the fact that you girls are going to be living with them. You know the rules. Don't let your guard down, don't accept anything from her. That goes for you as well Q. If she doesn't like one, then she doesn't like the other."

"That's exactly what I told her. She thinks she can befriend me, and have beef with my sister. It doesn't work like that. These chicks better recognize we are one!" Q roars.

"Your dad can not know about this because you know he would not allow you girls to move in with them. I'm not going to say anything, but I want updates. If it becomes a problem with you all, we will get an apartment for you two."

"Nah Ma, we're fine. I'm not worried about that girl." I say.

"I know you Zak. You hold on to grudges for long periods of time and I know you have something up your sleeve. Just remember, she may also have something up her sleeve. Always be two steps ahead."

"I will," I assure my mother.

After Mom's intervention, we yelled for daddy to come

downstairs and watch the movie with us. Daddy is so funny, him and Q are the comedians of the family. We even had a pillow fight until Mom got mad because Daddy hit her too hard with the pillow. On our last night home with our parents, Q and I cooked dinner, with Moms guidance of course.

We enjoyed the time we spent with our parents, but those three days went by so fast. The morning Q and I were leaving for school our parents walked us outside to the car and Daddy filled it with our things. We all gave each other long, tight hugs, we said our goodbyes.

Before we got on the road to college, we drove to Ms. B's house. Q wanted to say her goodbyes to her mom. Since Ms. B is not welcome to come to our house we went to her house. Once we got to Ms. B's house Q got out and went inside. I waited outside in the car. Ms. B walked Q out and waved to me. Q got in the car and we were off to college.

Q and I never discussed the relationship of our parents. We are well aware that Daddy cheated on my mom with Q's mom. It's complicated for us, so we don't talk about it at all. We're happy we were raised together and I'm quite sure it was hard for my mom. A lot of women wouldn't allow their cheating husband to bring his illegitimate child into their home, which is understandable but then children grow up not knowing their siblings.

We were having such a great time on the ride back to school. I drove and Q was the DJ. We were singing along to all our favorite songs. We arrived in record time.

Once we got to the house, I immediately called the Gucci store to have my clothes delivered. We awaited M and Irie's arrival. I'm not sure how they are going to act because I haven't seen them since the incident at the club. Q and I chose our bedrooms and quickly began to put our belongings away.

CHAPTER 8

MOVING ON UP

ZAK

Q and I arrived a day earlier than M and Irie. We wanted to pick our rooms first and leave them the others. We chose the larger rooms. Oh well, they should have gotten here first. We have a four-bedroom house and 2 and half bathrooms. All the bedrooms are upstairs with two on either side with its own bathrooms. The half bathroom is on the main floor along with a kitchen, dining room and living room and large office for us to study.

"You guys must have gotten here mighty early," M said once they arrived.

"No. We got here yesterday," Q announced.

"Oh, okay." M replied.

"Hi Zak. Hey Q." Irie spoke as she walked through the door with her bags.

Q and I spoke to Irie and walked into the dining room as they went upstairs to their bedrooms. They settled in and things seemed a little awkward. It was as if no one knew what to say to one another.

Irie apologized to me like she told Q she would. It sounded sincere but I know Irie is fake and phony as hell, so I played right along with her fake as apology. I accepted and told her we are good. I don't want tension in the house but I'm still fucking her up before she graduates and leaves. You know Q...she got it started.

"Awww shit you know what? They are going to be sweatin' us! You know we have to do a back-to-school night up in here," Q said excited.

"YOU KNOW I'M DOWN. I was thinking the same thing when we were driving here." Irie agrees with Q.

"We can hook it up. I'm gonna go make some flyers on the computer and we can pass them out."

We printed flyers and posted them in the cafeteria, handed them out and told others to spread the word. M and I went to the store for alcohol and snacks. Chips and pretzels were all they were getting. The word spread fast about the back-to-school party. Our house was packed by 9:30 that night. We did not charge a fee to get in, but we did charge for drinks. Q was our DJ for the night, bringing out her Bluetooth speaker and the music was blaring through our house. M was our bartender, Irie was our hype person, teaching everyone how to do her dance, and I was the hostess. The party was lit, we even met some people that have been there for a while, but new to us. I like to keep my circle extremely small. I think that has a lot to do with our up bringing. The less friends you have, then the less 'frenemies' you'll have also. The party was over around 2:30-3:00 in the morning and the house was a mess but thank god we hadn't bought furniture yet because I would be pissed off. We went to bed and decided we will clean up in the morning.

Everyone woke up to Irie yelling. "Y'all bitches better get up because I'm not cleaning this house up by myself."

We were so tired, nobody got out of bed. This bitch decides to start blasting music to force us up.

"Yo! Turn that shit down, we up," Q shouts over the loud music as she walked down the hall.

"Alright Irie! We're up and we're about to help you clean, but you gonna turn that shit down. I can barely hear myself talking," M yells.

"Okay I just wanted to make sure all you bitches were up. Oh by the way how are we splitting the money we made last night?" Irie questioned.

"What you mean how?" It's four of us, so we split that shit four ways." Q shouts.

"I really don't care how it's done," M halfheartedly replies as she places used cups into plastic garbage bags.

"The smart thing to do is make it the house money. We can buy groceries and furniture," I add to which they all agree.

After cleaning the house, we went shopping. M asked us to drive with them and we had no excuse not to this time. Music is what saved us because we didn't have to talk to one another. We all sang along to the songs playing on the radio. Once we got out of the car a little awkwardness lingered in the air. We shop for and agreed upon the living room and kitchen set. We agreed on the furniture quickly. There are two bathrooms of which Q and I will share one, while M and Irie share the other. Thanks to Moretti, I kindly pulled my black card to purchase the items Q and I need for the bathroom. While also purchasing our bedding and décor for both our bedrooms. After furniture shopping, we stop at the grocery store. We went our separate ways because everyone bought what they like to eat and again, I pull my black card to purchase me and Q's food.

We return to our house to start decorating. We put pictures on the walls, placed area rugs where needed and even painted an accent wall red in the living room. The tension seemed to die down a bit.

. . .

"DID EVERYONE GET THEIR SCHEDULE," I asked making conversation.

"My first class starts on Tuesday. They are from Tuesday – Thursday. I'm so happy because I didn't want my last year to be hectic, but technically I'm not done. I still have to go to law school," M explained.

"Yeah, I got mine. I have class every day except on Fridays. Don't feel bad M. I'm not done either. I still have to go to med school. You know I plan to be a plastic surgeon." I say.

"My goal is to be a nurse practitioner. I can practice under my sister. I'm done playing ball," Q throws her arms up as if to make a jump shot.

My classes start on Monday. I have classes five days a week, but I'm done by 10:30am on Fridays." Q explains.

"I want to be a corporate business owner. I have a double major in accounting and business. I have classes every day, but the way my schedule is, I will have a few free hours in between them," Irie tells them.

"Well, I hope we all accomplish our goals and be very successful," I say sincerely.

"Oh boy! Here she goes— getting all sentimental...enough already," Q said in between laughs.

Q's laughter catches on as everyone joins in, including me.

We all went back to putting the finishing touches on the house. Hopefully, the paint will dry before the furniture is delivered.

CHAPTER 9

ENTANGLEMENT
MOM

One night at the hospital, the ER was short-staffed so nurse Betty asked if I could come down and give them a hand. It wasn't like I had to rush home to my sweet husband because he wasn't there anyway. I complied with nurse Betty's request and agreed to do some overtime and work in the ER with her.

It was extremely busy that night. We had gunshot victims, car accidents, asthma attacks and everything else you could think of that would bring someone to the ER. One patient came in with shortness of breath and pain in his arm and chest so that needed our immediate attention. At that time, I was just leaving another patient's room when his entourage burst through the emergency doors, stating that he couldn't breathe. I immediately jumped into action and we took him into a private room to work on him. We drew blood, took his blood pressure, and did an EKG. We also took chest ex-rays. All procedural for someone coming in with his symptoms.

As the night began to calm down and all the patients were stabilized and cared for, I went back to the room to check on the patient who had shortness of breath. I really didn't take notice of how handsome he was because his health took precedence. Now that everything is calm, I can see clearly how gorgeous this specimen is.

"Who do I have the pleasure of helping me?" he asks trying to get my name even though it says it on my name tag.

"Nurse Monroe," I said.

"Well, you're very pretty Nurse Monroe."

I thank him and try not to blush. "How are you feeling now?" I ask.

"Better thanks to you. I may need your number in case shit hits the fan again," he smirks.

"We're very blunt, aren't we sir."

"Well, I may need a private duty nursing and I would love for Nurse Monroe to take care of me."

"Sorry, I don't do that."

"Well you can start with me. It's been a while, but about a year ago my doctor did suggest I get a visiting nurse. Let's just say I was a little reluctant. But if you're one of my choices, I'd be happy to make an exception. If you do come, not everyone knows about my...condition. We don't speak of it. And you won't either."

"Again, that's just not what I do, sir."

"I'll make sure it's worth it...I can draw up a contract for three times a week," he pursues before looking in the direction of his henchmen. "Give me paper and a pen." He turns back to face me. "I'm sure a nurse wouldn't allow a guy with a bad heart to go without good care."

God, this guy just won't let up. He must not be used to rejection. I can see already that his looks must get him pretty far with the ladies until he opens his damn mouth. I need to get out of here. "I'll think about it."

He smiles handing me the piece of paper with his name, address, phone number and the outrageous amount he's willing to pay for it. This arrogant ass is out of his mind. "This is an awful lot of money to pay me for three days a week sir."

"Well as they say, good help is hard to find. So, since I've found it, I should pay well to get it and keep it."

The amount may have nudged me toward accepting his offer, but I still needed to think about this. "I have to check on my other patients. I'll give you a call if this becomes acceptable."

I got home late that night and my husband was nowhere to be found, nor did he call all day to check on me. He doesn't even know I worked late. From the looks of things, it seems as though he never came home. Well, I guess he's up to his old self again, either staying out late or not coming home at all. He put on a good show while the girls were home from school but as soon as they left, he was back to his usual....and must have rather spent time with his women.

I can't believe I put up with his shit for all these years. This is not the person my parents raised me to be. They raised me to be strong, but my husband makes me weak. I accept and tolerate shit that I never thought I would. This is the last straw he needs to get his shit together or get out. I can do bad all by myself.

Zak called home to check on us.

"Hey Mom. How are you guys?" she asked. "I don't mean to call so late but I called earlier and no one answered."

I take a deep breath, ready to lie to my daughter. "Oh, your dad's at work and I'm home watching a movie." My daughter and I have a pretty good relationship, so we can tell when one is bullshitting the other.

"Seriously Mom. How are you really doing? You sound depressed or something."

I really don't want her to worry about things she shouldn't have to. What goes on between her father and me should not be in her thoughts right now. So, I try to add a bit more excitement in my voice. "Zak, everything's fine." I know she's not going to believe me, but I hope she doesn't press the issue.

She doesn't. "How are things at the house with the other girls?"

She takes a deep breath, "As good as expected I guess."

"You just remember what I said. Don't trust that Irie girl."

"I know Mom. She tries to play nice, but I can see right through that fake phony smile of hers."

"I'm glad you're paying attention. Look out for your sister and send her my love."

We hung up because she had another call coming through.

————————————————

Zak

WHEN I HUNG up with my mom to answer the other call, I recognized the voice immediately to be Morretti. I was excited to hear his sexy voice, but I didn't let him know. He told me he was making plans for us to meet because he wanted to see me. My insides were screaming yes because the anticipation was inevitable. We made plans for the upcoming Friday night. I would drive to meet him at the same hotel he left the black card a few weeks ago. That was two hours away from the college.

It seems as though the week went by extremely fast. The time has come for me to put up or shut up. I have been talking a lot of shit to Moretti about him being able to keep up with me sexually. Now it's time to show and prove. Of course, I let Q know where I was going and all the info. After being sure that this is really what I wanted to do, she just told me to be careful.

When I arrived at the hotel, I did valet parking, walked inside and I noticed how gorgeous (beautiful) it was. The lobby's décor was gorgeous. Green and white marble floors and crystal chandeliers hung throughout. My first time there I was in and out so fast I didn't notice. I retrieved the key from the receptionist and headed to the room. I wore a large hat with shades not to be recognized. When the elevators doors opened, I felt nervous. I want to turn around to leave because I began to feel guilty because he's married and he's my friend's father. I quickly pushed those feelings aside and continue down the hall. No turning back now.

As I apprehensively opened the door, the fresh smell of candles and roses hit my nose before I even saw them. The room was dimly lit as the ambience of the rose petals on the floor and the candles displayed around the room calmed my nerves instantly. Moretti must have heard me enter the room, because he called out to tell me he'd be right out. I walked in a little further, removing my hat and sunglasses, taking in the fact that he did all this for me. Either he really wanted to get in my pants, or he wanted to make me feel special. Although I'm sure it's my first thought, I don't mind pretending that he did this to ease my apprehension.

I hear the door to the bathroom open and see Moretti walk into the living room where I was standing. He's shirtless, showing the sexiness of his chiseled abs taking me right back to the first time I saw him. Is it possible for him to look even better now? I feel my middle twitch and the wetness seep through my panties as he walks closer toward me. Without a word, he gently grabs my face in his strong hands and caresses his lips against mine. Spreading my mouth slightly with his wet tongue, he proceeds to press against my lips more firmly. Our first kiss. It was soft and sensual but meaningful. My heart fell to my chest as and my knees buckled a little. I was more nervous than I thought. He stops unexpectedly to stare down at me to make sure he's not pressuring me, I guess. I just smile slightly encouraging him to continue, because clearly, I might be enjoying this embrace much more than expected.

I had to get it together quickly before I lost my cool. I had to be in control, and I was not feeling that way at the moment. I abruptly excused myself and took off my coat and then went into the bathroom to catch my breath. I splashed cold water on my face and dried it with the hand towel hanging on the rack. I stood in the bathroom a few moments longer to calm my nerves. I stared at myself in the mirror, telling myself that I'm the one with the upper hand. I'm a fucking woman. We're always the ones in control.

"I hope you're hungry because I took the liberty of ordering dinner for us. I chose lobster, steak, pasta and broccoli," he said as soon as I walked back into the room.

"Sure, but after that kiss we could've skipped dinner."

He smiles, tilting his head to the side to eye me curiously. "I see," he says simply. He walks slowly toward me, staring directly into my eyes. He stops right in front of me, place his hands behind his back and leans forward. Now he's directly in front of my face, lips barely touching. "I think you should eat first. You're going to need it." He kisses me softly once more before grabbing my hand and leading me to the couch. "Tell me a little about Zakkiya." Moretti says to me as we sat on the couch.

The first thing he wanted to know was if I were pleased with the house he purchased for us. He also asked what my plans after graduation were. He informed me that I can use the black card at my leisure. We also talked about me going to med school and that his line of work was construction. He caressed my hands the entire time we talk, complimenting my looks and the scent of my perfume.

Room service came about thirty minutes later. We sat at the table to eat, and to my surprise, the food was excellent. He pours us a glass of wine before going back over to the couch. He removed my shoes and began to massage my feet and legs. His hands were strong yet soft on my skin. It felt so tantalizing my legs slightly spread involuntarily inviting his touch. He was really paying attention to my entire body and knew exactly what to touch to get me aroused.

He takes the glass of wine from my grasp and quickly kisses me all over. He sucked my neck gently as his strong hands rub my breasts, before picking me up and carrying me over to the king size bed. Gently placing me on the soft bed, he continues to massage my body. He begins to slowly remove every piece of clothing I have on, taking his time and never losing eye contact...making me want him even more. The walls of my pussy pulsate, and I want him inside of me right at that moment. As he stood to remove his clothes I stared at him, slithering two of my tiny fingers inside of my wet, ready pussy. His eyes widen at the sight of my seduction as he squeezes his hardened dick in his palm. To tease further, I remove my fingers from my dripping warmth and taste my own juices. With that, he finally jerks his pants down, letting his dick fling making me want to sit on his engorged dick.

I was ready, but I had to keep my composure and be a big girl, because I'm playing a big girl's game. My thoughts are rambling on, *should I give him all of me or should I hold back?* The way he has me feeling I'm probably going to give him all of me.

"I'm jealous," he whispers as he licks his lips at the sight of me licking my finger.

He spins me onto my stomach and yanks me up to lift my ass in the air. Before I know it, he's shoving his tongue deep in my dripping folds, using his mouth to fuck me from behind. I grabbed at the sheets trying to keep my composure never feeling such pleasure in my short sexual life. If this is what being with a grown ass man is like, there's no way I'll be able to stay away from him. I began to move my lower body against his face, indulging in his writhing hunger. He growls into me as he grabs onto my thighs excited that he's doing exactly what I need. The urge to call him daddy comes over me, but I fight the desire. I held out from giving him that much control. The way he has me feeling, further confirms he is a grown ass man that didn't come to play games.

He worked my body over so well I felt dizzy. When he turned me back over, he asked if I was okay, but now it's my turn. Not a time for talking.

"Get on your back," I command.

I watch him as he complies and I grab his large dick, pulling it back to make his jewels completely visible. I pull them into my mouth as I squeeze his shaft. I stare at his face as he watches intently, silently begging for me to continue. That one move sending him reeling immediately. I let my now very wet tongue slither up his dick as he makes his O face and I swallow him whole. He damn near loses it right then and there but grabs at the sheets and closes his eyes to try and hold on as I deep throat his full hard dick completely. It doesn't take long before he explodes into my mouth.

I waste no time in hopping on top of him to make sure I ride him better than any woman he's ever met, He yells out uncontrollably, my name bouncing off these hotel walls like a little boy crying for help. I slow my pace just a little because I can feel him shake. I'm not ready to cum so I turn on his dick and ride him backwards, with my ass in his face. He palms both my ass cheeks and squeeze tightly. I ride up and down his dick so good you can hear the sex sounds my juices were making. I couldn't hold out any longer and told him to cum with me. Again, his moans and groans can be heard throughout the room. I bit down on my lip to try not to scream, it felt so good a little moan escapes my mouth.

"I gotta go, I have a two-hour ride ahead of me," I remind him.

"You're leaving? You should stay."

"I can't, I have a lot of studying to do," I lie not wanting him to think he's got it like that.

"I guess I'll go too then. No need staying here alone," he

said as I gathered my things to shower first. While in the shower I had time to myself to reflect on what just happened. It was absolutely amazing. I'm tingling all over and I can't wait to tell Q because I'm about to burst with excitement. Fuck M and her momma! I laughed out, but quickly realize I could have possibly just ruined a friendship...a family.

After my shower, I suggest we leave out separately and for him to wait thirty minutes before he left. He watched as I put my incognito clothing on, and he gave a little chuckle.

"I have to be extra careful, you never know who's watching," I explain to Moretti.

"I understand. Goodnight Zakkiya." He says.

I waited for valet to pull my car around. I was more nervous leaving than I was when I arrived at the hotel. I look around because it feels as if I'm being watched. I know it's my nerves getting the best of me, but the hairs on my neck literally stood as chills crept up my back. I turned to look but I don't see anyone. I'm so glad to see my car pull up, I walk to the driver's side door before the valet could get out. I gave him a fifty-dollar tip and he was more than pleased.

"Thank you, ma'am." He says smiling, as I waved and pulled off.

Of course, Q waited up for me to hear all the details.

Thank God this house has two bedrooms on either side, but just to make sure we're not heard, I close my door and still whisper.

"Sissy this motherfucka is different!" I tell her with an excited whisper and smiling from ear to ear.

"He screamed my name and wanted me to stay." I tell Q.

"Good move I'm glad you didn't." Q says.

"Girl he's fucking hung like a horse. No wonder his wife don't play no games. He got something special down there." I shake my head and smile while reminiscing of my night.

"I need the hook up with his brother, cousin uncle, some-body shit." Q says and they both bust out in laughter.

"Goodnight sissy. I'm about to call him to let him know I made it home safely." I say to Q before I walk out of her room.

"Goodnight." Q says.

Meeting him on Friday nights became a habit. He offered to buy me a home as a graduation present. I think I was just as hooked as he was, but I will always play as if he's just average. I know he could never be mine solely because he's married. This is just a sexcapade for me and I can't catch feelings.

CHAPTER 10

IRIE'S SECRET
ZAK

Time is really going by fast at school. With our busy schedules, we hardly saw each other, except for on the weekends. Even though Irie doesn't say much to me, I can tell she is still holding a grudge against me. Her resentment doesn't matter to me, I play it cool and act like everything is fine between us. The other day she walked pass me and if I didn't speak I don't think she would have. Maybe I'm overthinking it. As I finish getting dressed I hear Q yell for us to come downstairs.

I went to the kitchen where Q was preparing breakfast for us all. Since we weren't eating anything Irie cooked, we must do it ourselves. We'll always remember when Irie mixed her feces in oxtail gravy. No thank you.

Q made waffles, eggs, and bacon. She displayed platters of food for us buffet style. I poured glasses of orange juice for all of us. As I was making my plate M walks in with a big smile on her face, which I'm glad because I wasn't sure how either one of them were going to act this morning.

"What the hell you are smiling so hard for?" Q asked as she too was smiling.

"I'm happy as hell you cooked. I'm hungry as shit." M said laughing while

fixing her plate.

"Good morning, what y'all laughing for?" Irie says entering the kitchen.

"We're laughing at M's greedy ass. She's happy I cooked" Q responds.

"Me too! My stomach is growling' and shit." Irie admits as she piles food on her plate.

"I can tell, with your grown man plate." I say.

They all bust out laughing and it became easier to converse after the jokes.

As we were eating, I realized then, this is the first time Irie talked about her family. She told us how special the holidays are to her and her family, so she always goes home for the holidays with her Auntie and Uncle. She also adds that she doesn't have much family living here in Jersey because most of them are in Jamaica. Her mom, sister and brother are in Jamaica, but her cousins who are from Virginia will be visiting this year.

Q and I both had this questionable look on our faces, obviously thinking the same thing.

"I didn't know you had family in Virginia. You never mentioned that to us," Q interrogates.

"Actually, I told you guys at the club that I knew ole' boy from Virginia, but everything went left, and we never talked about it."

I notice M shift in her seat and looks up at Q, remembering she had punched Irie that night. Q gives M a look as if to say oh well Bitch better come correct.

Irie takes notice of the looks but doesn't say anything else about the night at the club. She then continues to say when she was eleven and still living in Jamaica, a family member molested her. Although the creep went to jail, she didn't want to be there anymore because everyone knew what happened.

Irie's eyes begin to well with tears, as she relives the events in her mind. She paused and took a deep breath to prevent the tears from falling down her face.

"My mom sent me to live with my family in Virginia, but when he got out of jail, he also moved to Virginia with other family members of mine. I really don't talk about them because that's fucked up that they took him in knowing what he did to me. Again, not wanting to stay in the same town where he resides, I moved to Jersey with my Auntie May and Uncle Carl when I was a junior in high school.

I only deal with my family that I lived with in Virginia— they always had my back," she confides. As Irie tells her story, we all have sad expressions on our faces, M reaches over to grab Irie's hand to console her.

Irie continues. "That's how I know your friend Kareem. He's good friends with my cousins and he always came to the house to visit them. When I moved here to Jersey, he always hit me up whenever he came to visit."

"Wow, this is a small world, but nah. I didn't know that. I wouldn't fuck with them either. I'm sorry that happened to you," Q said.

"Yeah, Irie, I'm sorry too. That's so messed up, especially a family member doing that shit," I say sincerely.

"They try and pretend like it never happened, but it had me fucked up as a kid. I made a promise to myself that I was going to kill his ass. He's walking around living his best life as if he never did that to me," Irie blurts before closing her eyes to calm her anger but is unable to contain it. "Do you know he has a wife and kids now? I bet they don't know he is a child molester. My plan is to expose his ass real soon."

"What are your plans to expose his ass, cause I hate bitch ass motherfuckers like that." M says ready to help her friend.

"Yeah I'll print some pictures of his ass and post them all over with child molester typed under his name." Q chimed in.

"No, seriously Irie. What do you want to do to expose his ass? I'm ready whenever you're ready." I say wholeheartedly.

"I appreciate y'all because this is the first time I've talked about it since I was a kid. My family act like it's a big secret. Instead of getting me help, my family sent me to Virginia as if that was therapy. I didn't talk about it at all because it really had me fucked up." Irie wipes away the tears that she couldn't prevent from falling.

Today was the first time I saw a softer side of her. It was like her vulnerability humanized her in a way. We all just sat there thinking of a way to console her. Everyone continuously gave their apologies before we simultaneously get up to give her a hug. I really feel bad for Irie because that's the worse thing a kid has to deal with.

"Can we talk about something else because I hate to even think about it?" Irie pleaded.

We sat down at the table and began to eat in silence. It was a real awkward moment, because neither of us knew what to say after that. I mean what could we really say after that. Someone who was just punched in the face by my sister, and I plotted my revenge on just relived something I wouldn't want to happen to my worst enemy. Luckily M decides to break the silence and breaks my personal commiserating.

"Zak, did you say your cousins were visiting for the holidays? M asks.

"Yes all of them are coming. My Auntie is also coming." I responds with a smile on my face.

"Okay. Let's make sure we all hook up so we can meet your cousins from Virginia," M suggests.

"I'm going to find out exactly when they are coming up and we can hang out. I'm letting you know now, my cousins look good and I'm not hooking nobody up 'cause if it doesn't work out you can't blame me for nothing. If you'll want to hook up with one of my cousins, you are on your own." I laugh out loud as I explain to M and Irie.

They all laugh as they finished eating, turning the emotional morning into a more cheerful one. Irie picks up her phone to call her Auntie May. She speaks to her briefly turning on that Jamaican accent that she so easily turns off most of the time. When she ends the call, she informs us that her family is having a pre-Christmas celebration and she wants us to come see how Jamaicans party...Rastafarian style.

"Let's see if y'all can really hang because we party for days," Irie says with a huge smile on her face.

"Oh yeah! I can't wait, they party like rock stars," M squeals. "Well, speaking of parties, Irie and I are planning to have a huge graduation party."

"It's October and you talking about graduation," Q interjects.

"Shut up Q! You know how fast time flies. We need to book a hall and plan this right because it's going to be epic!" M says excitedly.

"I'm just messing with you. I know that's something that takes time and strategic planning," Q says.

CHAPTER 11

PAST GHOSTS

TONY

"Hey B, it's time for me to head home. I really been here with you for three days straight. It's just a matter of time before the girls will realize that I've been staying here. I don't want to have to explain that to them, nor do I want to hurt them. It's bad enough that I have been with you almost the entire time I've been with my wife," I say while putting on my shoes to leave.

"Well, I told you before I'm not going anywhere. I don't even want to be a wife. I'm fine with what we have. I don't think I ever want to be married because I would have killed you by now," Beatrice responds as she stands in front of him with her hand on her hip.

"I love my wife, but it's just so complicated." I shake my head in disbelief. "You know how to relate to me and my upbringing. Sheila was raised differently from you and I, and I don't know if she would have accepted my lifestyle. That's why I didn't tell her when I met her," I drop my head, "and then it never felt right to tell her at all. It was as if I let her down. She's the reason I got a legitimate job. So, if she ever checked, at least that would be the truth."

"You're right we were raised in the same neighborhood, but

I'm hood rich now," she says as she throws money up in the air. The money that Steven had placed on the dresser for her, something he does every time he comes to visit her. Money lands on the bed and some on the floor. "I never had to work, and you always took care of me."

"I don't know why you think that's okay, you should have at least gotten an education," I say as I stand, snatching money from the bed. "All the money I have given you could have paid for college five times." Frustrated I throw the money in her face. "You are excellent with figures. You could have gone to school for accounting or something, but you rather sit and wait for me to provide for you and then say it like it's okay." I grab my coat and head to the door.

"I don't know what the hell is wrong with you all of a sudden!" she says following closely behind. "Yes, you can go home to your educated wife because I don't have to put up with your bullshit. Get the fuck out of my house and come back when you know how to talk to me," she yells as she mushes his head back with her fingers.

I yell back somewhat pissed that she just put her hands on me. "You mean my house! And yes, my wife is highly educated. Goodbye B!" I slam the door so hard, it sounds as if the two pictures she has hanging on the wall beside the door, fall to the floor.

I need to clear my mind, because it seems like everything is getting the best of me. I'm still hiding out from Moretti, I'm cheating on my wife for no apparent reason, and my mom still isn't talking to me. Not to mention I haven't seen my parents in eight years.

I get in the car, grabbing hard at the steering wheel upset that I let that happen. I'm not sure what I'm more mad at. The fact that we said those things to each other or that she mushed me. She fucking mushed me. I start the engine to my BMW. I start to drive down the road and just keep on going without a destination in mind. I'm not sure how long I was driving, but it must have been at least two hours. My gaslight came on, so I pulled over to the nearest gas station, then went inside the convenient store attached it. I bought a soda, a bag of chips and paid for my gas. When I came out, another car was right next to mine getting gas. As I walked pass the car, the guy got out the car and said, "Tony!" I almost stopped in my tracks, but I played it off and acted like I was picking up something off the ground. I never looked at the guy when I came out of the store because I wasn't expecting any one to recognize me. The guy proceeded to jog over to me and say, "Hey Tony! It's me Hector."

I looked at him confused. "Sorry sir. My name is not Tony, you have the wrong guy."

"C'mon Tony. I know that's you. We go way back, and we were close as hell, so you can't tell me you're not Tony." He takes a step back, I guess to show he's not approaching to cause trouble. "Look man, I know you moved away to get away from Mr. Moretti, but I still have love for you man. We grew up together."

I walk up to Hector, grab him by the arm and walk into the store near the back door.

"Are you following me?" I ask as I glance around the store agitated.

"Did Moretti tell you to look for me? Does he have a hit out on me?" I bombard Hector with questions.

"Man, you know I would never do anything to hurt you. Yes, Moretti has a hit out on you and your brother James, but no one has ever seen you two," he puts his head down, "so he said that the hit still remains no matter how long it takes."

I release Hector's arm and relax a little. If he wanted me dead, he would have done it considering I didn't even know it was Hector in the car.

"The only reason I still work for Moretti is because he knows too much about my family and I know if I left, he would have killed them. He would think I turned on him for you and you brothers. I stayed so I could get close as I could to him and learn the business," he says glancing around the store wanting to remain inconspicuous. "You were smart not to let him know anything about your personal life. All Moretti knows about you is your parents and two brothers and that you moved your parents away. I wish I had followed in your footsteps."

I continue to look around the store as Hector is talking. I know I need to get out of here and I need to do it carefully. I want to know what the hell Moretti does or doesn't know.

"It was only my Grams and three sisters. I was the only man in the house, so I had to take care of them. I had to make money quick I'll never forget..." Hector reminisces, sincerity in his voice. "We were sixteen when I asked you to introduce me to Moretti so I could work for him. You told me no, 'cause you didn't want me to work for him because he was the devil. I told you we needed groceries, so you went to the store and bought $300 worth of food for my house and gave my grams $500 in an envelope. You told her it was from your parents because you knew she wouldn't accept it from you, because we were the same age."

I finally start to believe that Hector is not following me and it's a mere coincidence that he ran into me.

"You also told me you would always look out for me and you did. I wanted to feel like a man and provide for my own family. So, what did I do? Tell you if you didn't introduce me, I would go to him on my own. Moretti crossed the line!" Hector inadvertently yells, then lowers his voice as he looks around the store to make sure no one heard him. "He started using my younger sister's house to stash his drugs and money. My sister was doing this for years for him and I never said anything to Moretti. I went to my sister and asked her why the hell would she get involved with Moretti and she told me she was grown she can make her own choices. I tried to talk to her, but she wouldn't listen." Hector shakes his head as he continues to tell his story as I listened. "The word on the streets was that she started stealing Moretti's money because he stopped paying her. She had two little kids to take care of and I know she would do anything to provide for them. I spoke to her the morning of the day she was killed. She told me she had to tell me something, so I said I'll come to her that evening." Hector's voice starts to become shaky as he tells the rest of his story. I knew it couldn't have been easy for him. "By the time I got to her house, the coroners were taking my sister's body out in a body bag. I ran into the house because they were about to call DCFS to come get my niece and nephew. My sister must have known something, or she was about to leave because the baby's diaper bag was packed and also a bag packed for my nephew. I'm not sure if my nephew saw who killed his mom, but they were in the house when it happened, so I know he at least heard it. I promise on my life, I'm not going to rest until I find out who did it and they are all dead. I know Moretti had everything to do with this. I also want to know which one of his flunkies killed my sister."

"Yeah, I heard about that on the news and the first thing that popped into my head was Moretti had something to do with that. I wanted to reach out to you so bad but didn't want to chance it. The day of your sister's funeral I drove pass just to see you. I wanted to get out, but I didn't know if Moretti or his flunkies would be there."

"I'm so glad to see you Tony." Hector suddenly embraces me with a manly hug. "I really want to get Moretti, but I don't trust any of them dudes. They will snitch on me so fast and I'll be dead before I could blink my eyes. You're the only person I can trust."

"Of course, I got your back, but we have to plan this the right way. My family is good, and he don't know where we live. It's time I pay him back for what he put my family through too."

Hector and I exchanged numbers. I gave Hector the number to my phone that's under a fake company name. I believe him, but I always have to be cautious. We said our good-byes quickly and told me that he'll call. All I can hope is that I just didn't make a big fucking mistake.

CHAPTER 12

THAT "B" IS OUT

SHEILA

"Oh, so you decided to come home," I say in a sarcastic tone.

"Yea Sheila. I needed a break to clear my mind," my supposed husband replies as he hangs his coat in the closet.

"I'm sick of your shit! You stay gone for three days straight and you walk through my damn door as if everything is just fine." I inch closer to him, "You can have all the breaks you need. I'm going out." I walk pass him and start putting my coat on. Before my husband could stop me, I'm out the door and in my car.

I really need someone to vent to. Tony has us so secluded and I wasn't raised this way. My family is very close, and we shared our feelings with each other as a way of getting sound advice. Once I married Tony however, I couldn't have friends, no one could come over and I definitely couldn't talk about him to anyone. It's crazy how I willingly let him upend my life with no hesitation. I sit behind the steering wheel of my car, staring at the front door when it hits me. I just walked out of the house and my husband didn't come after me. There are so many times I wondered if he still loves me.

I called Betty to see if she would like any company and she

informed me that she and the other nurses were going out. Sounds like a plan to me. Obviously, my husband doesn't give a shit what I do. I'm upset my husband didn't come after me, but I have to get my emotions in check. I can't let my colleagues see me this way. I turn the music on in my car to uplift my spirits before I get there. When I walked in to meet them for dinner and drinks, I noticed how lovely the lounge was. Dimly lit and very pleasing to the eye. They shared a booth in the corner with a small light hanging above. Betty waved me over as she notices me as I walk in. The expressions on their faces couldn't hide what they are thinking. They are in complete shock that I even showed up. This is only my third time going out with them within the seven years of working together. They are constantly joking around, saying my husband has me on lock down and I can't come out to play.

"Sue I'm glad you came out with us. We've been joking, laughing, and enjoying each other's company since the day we met. We have to do this more often, well you need to come out with us more often." Patricia says.

At that moment, our waiter walked over to our table with a drink in hand. He placed the drink in front of me stating the guy at the bar says to bring this over to the beautiful lady.

I held the drink up to the guy at the bar, nodded my head and mouthed thank you.

The waiter cleared our table before he walks away.

"No wonder your husband don't let you out, he knows the men be sweatin' you." Louise says as they all share a laugh.

I have to say I really enjoyed myself with the other ladies. I might have needed to be around other women who I might be able to relate to. They were all there and willing to loosen me up. Patricia is the Head Nurse on the maternity ward. Louise is the Head Nurse in Pediatrics. Betty is the Head Nurse in the E.R. and me, the Head Nurse in the O.R.

We all met seven years ago when I start working at the

hospital. I recall eating my lunch alone in the employees lounge of the hospital. Betty, Patricia, and Louise ate together each day at the same time. Always laughing and have a great time with one another. On this particular day, their laughs were so contagious I started to laugh not knowing what I was laughing at. They invited me over to their table and here we are seven years later still colleagues and now friends. We ate and had drinks and drank some more. We talked about our jobs, family, and love life. However, the same information we tell the girls to share is the same information I have to. No different. No one knows where I live. All they know is I have two daughters and a husband. That's all they are going to know.

Not long after our chatter, we finish our drinks and Patricia and Louise said their goodbyes.

Betty and I lingered around talking a little while longer. I feel the closest to Betty, although she's single and always ready to mingle. She makes it seem as though not being married is the best way to be. I somewhat believe her because my husband has been cheating on me since before we got married. Obviously I've lost my mind letting someone treat me like that.

As our conversation grows deeper, she lets me know that she's fully aware that I'm not happy in my relationship.

"The other ladies may not be able to see through your fake smiles, but I can," Betty explains, then takes a deep breath. "I've been in your shoes for many years. I was not always single. I was married and my ex-husband constantly cheated on me, and mentally and physically abused me."

"I'm so sorry to hear that Betty."

"It's ok I've moved on from him and that horrible marriage, but all of this took place while I was taking care of his four children. Mind you, I never had any kids of my own and two of his children were conceived while married to me." Her eyes widen before she rolls them and shakes her head. "I finally had enough courage to leave him. I went to school and became a nurse and here I am now— enjoying life to the fullest."

"I have thought about leaving on several occasions. I stay mainly because of the girls," I reason. I really wish I could fully confide in her about exactly what's going on in my frustrating life, but as much as I know my husband is unfaithful, I refuse to tell her the whole truth.

"Hello! Sue, are you listening to me?" Betty inserts herself into my self-pity.

"Yes Betty. I'm listening. I just have so much on my mind right now. I heard everything you were saying. It's just that some things I must handle on my own," Sue admitted.

"I understand. I'm here if you ever need me. I'm just a phone call away."

"You know what Betty? I would like to take you up on your offer. I don't want to go home tonight so can I crash at your house?"

"Of course, you can. I have a spare bedroom and it's all yours." Betty's smile is bright as the sun. She's pleased I finally let her in.

We left the lounge for Betty's house. For some reason, as I followed her in my car, a feeling of freedom washed over me. Something I hadn't felt for many years. Tony has never raised his hand to me but who's to say what will happen now that I'm not going home tonight. I'm the one not giving a shit, and finally putting my needs before his.

We arrived at Betty's house and as soon as I walked in, I noticed she has a very lovely home. Exceptionally clean and decorated beautifully. It's a two bedroom two-and-a-half-bathroom townhouse. She showed me to the spare room and told me to make myself comfortable. I felt the urge to thank her once again, to which she responds to just think of her home as a home away from home. Something I am all too eager to experience, especially tonight. So much so, I even turned my phone off for the night. I hadn't slept so soundly in years. I close my eyes off to the drama of my life and whatever hell will come tomorrow.

The next morning I wake up feeling refreshed as the sunbeams warm my face. I stretch across the bed with a wide smile looking around my home away from home as if I never wanted to leave. I do actually have a life and I'm pretty sure a pissed off husband. As they say, what's good for the goose is good for the gander. I turn on my side and stare at the phone, dreading having to turn the damn thing on. Sadly I must. No sooner than the sounds of the phone powering on, do I hear the constant barrage of messages. I stare at the screen seeing that my husband left twenty-three messages. A slight grin of satisfaction comes over my face as I now see that he still does feel at something for the woman he promised to cherish all those years ago. I started to play them back, each message basically saying the same.

"Sheila, where are you? Call me as soon as you get my message."

I have mixed emotions. One, it felt good that I was giving him a dose of his own medicine. On the other hand, I felt bad because he sounded worried and sad. I decide to deliberately go home late that afternoon. This is the first time I've ever stayed out overnight without my husband. When I walk in the door, I was expecting him to yell, fuss and fight with me but it was the total opposite. He looked so worried that his hair was disheveled. He must have been up all night according to the times of the messages. I could tell he was also drinking— something he never does. Initially, I felt bad that I played his game. Honestly, he has to get a taste of his own medicine. He grabbed and hugged me so tight as the tears fell from his eyes. I've never seen him cry. I literally pulled away from him to see for myself if this was real. I was in such disbelief.

"I thought something happened to you. I thought you were dead. Please don't ever do that to me again," he pleads.

"I had to give you a taste of your own medicine. You stayed out for three days without calling me or saying anything. The fear no longer sets in when you stay out because it has become the norm. I'm tired of you cheating and disappearing on me. I've even contemplated leaving you. The girls are grown now and only have a year and a half left in college. Then it will be time for me to worry about myself. I love you, but I love me more," I blurt out quickly before I lose my resolve.

He cups my face in his hands, "Sheila you know I love you with my whole heart. You allowed me to do whatever I wanted, and it just became easy for me. You never complained or even asked me to stop cheating. A man will do what a man wants if it's allowed. You are the best thing that ever happened to me. You raised both of my daughters into classy respectable young ladies." He pauses briefly and takes a deep breath before placing his forehead on mine. "It's time we have our talk about my past life. I'm going to tell you everything," he says then quickly leads me into the living room to sit on the couch.

CHAPTER 13

MY SECRET IS BIGGER
THAN YOURS
TONY

A s I walk my wife to the couch, a flutter of emotions comes over me. The main one being her just getting up and walking out that door without another word. I've been lying to her since the day we fucking met, why would she stay? Lord knows I haven't given her any reason to stay except a daughter that came from her womb, and another that came from my mistress's. That never stopped her from treating Q any differently. She's an amazing woman, and I'm just not prepared to lose her. For once, I need to not think about myself and do what's best for her.

"Okay Sheila, come sit beside me." *Here we go.* "As a kid I grew up in Newark. My dad was one of the biggest drug lords in Jersey and the surrounding states. He had a partner name Francesco Moretti, Sr. Moretti Sr. is an Italian mobster who ran the town where we grew up and other areas as well. Being that me and Moretti Jr. were friends, and our dads were close, they decided to teach us the drug game." I pause to see if I should continue. She stares back at me intently eager for me to finish. She closes her eyes briefly, and visibly relaxes before she reopens them. She stares quietly ready for me to continue.

"I know that I never told you before, but I have two brothers, Phil & James." Sheila sat with an even more stunned look on her face.

"My dad always told us not to get involved in the Moretti's personal lives and don't let them in ours. The Moretti's only know about my parents and siblings. Nobody knows that I'm married with two daughters. They also only knew about Beatrice."

At the mention of Ms. B's name, Sheila gives me a look that sends chills up my spine.

"I'm sorry honey but let me explain. She was someone I used from time to time. She kept my drugs and money for years and one day, she tells me she's pregnant."

"I see you mix business with pleasure," Sheila says as she shifts in her seat.

"I don't love Beatrice. I love you, but she is the mother of my other daughter, so that's why I moved her here after we moved."

Sheila stands to fix herself a drink because this conversation is clearly getting too heavy for her. I wait patiently, watching her every move, until she sits back down so I can continue.

I take a deep breath and clear my throat, somewhat pleased that she has a drink to soothe the next blow. "One night me and my two brothers had a job to do for Moretti. We were to take out this guy that was doing business in one of Moretti's areas without his permission. My brother Phil was tired of doing Moretti's dirty work. He would argue that we were all supposed to be partners. How was it that we've been working for him. He never gets his hands dirty and Phil felt it was time to show him he needs to step up to the plate. My other brother James and I tried to tell him it was not a good idea. Phil was adamant about it.

Instead of Phil driving to the location where we should have done the job, he drove us to a hotel to lay low. He was our brother and we were all in with him. Even though we knew the outcome wouldn't be good. The plan was for us to tell Moretti that the guy was not there that night and we would take care of the job later." Sheila was so into my story she downed her drink placing her empty glass on the coffee table. She sat back with folded arms with a look of interest on her face.

"Phil left me and James at the hotel," I drop my gaze to the floor. "He went to Moretti's house without us. A friend of ours named Hector told me that Mr. Moretti Jr. had my brother killed. Hector was a close friend of mine. He grew up on my block and reluctantly I brought him in to work for Mr. Moretti. Hector told me when Phil came to the house that night and told Moretti Jr. that me and James was going to complete the hit, but he wasn't his flunky, and he wasn't doing anymore dirt for him. They began arguing back and forth, and Moretti Jr. walked out and went into another room. When Phil walked in the room he was still yelling back and forth with Moretti. Hector said Moretti kept saying, 'you didn't complete the hit', and Moretti kept asking Phil about his money. Phil told him he didn't have any of his money."

"Did your brother take his money?" she asks suspiciously.

"Let me finish babe," I say anxious to finally get this off my chest. "Hector told me that Moretti continued yelling and saying that Phil has 2.5 million dollars of his and he wants it. Moretti accused James and me of having it if Phil didn't. Of course Phil defended us and said none of us had his money." I stand and start to pace the floor, as I relive my own personal hell. "Moretti's flunkies came inside the room and had Phil surrounded. Moretti's younger daughter Maria was peeking in the room. Moretti told his little girl to come in and he made some speech to her about being a boss and told her to shoot my brother in the head...she did it. Moretti made his daughter kill my brother."

"Did he really make his daughter kill someone?" she asks in disgust.

"That's what Hector said. Moretti is the devil himself and cares for no one. I know he loves his daughter. Honestly, I was shocked about that part." I drop my head in disgrace as I think about him telling his own daughter to do something like that. I would never want to see my daughter's in such a position. "At first, I didn't know what money he was talking about because if Phil did take Moretti's money, he didn't tell me or James about it. We certainly knew we had to get out of town. We knew he wouldn't or couldn't do anything to my parents, but me and my brothers were a different story. He'd have us shot in the head without a second thought. Thankfully, my brothers and I had a place where we stashed weapons, so we went to get them right away. But...when we got there...we saw a duffle bag full of fucking money. It had to be Moretti's."

"Oh, so he did take the money," she interrupts.

"Yes, he did," I respond shamefully. "We were not about to go ring Moretti's doorbell and say here's your money. So, we split it three ways. Me and James then I took a 3rd of the money to my Dad that night." I sit back down beside my wife and grab her hand into mine. "That's the reason I moved you all in the middle of the night. I already bought this house for us for reasons such as that. I told James to come with us, but he refused. He said it would be easier if we were apart. My brother went completely underground. I have not heard from him since that night and it's been almost eight years. I know he's all right cause he can take care of himself...I wish he would reach out to me."

Sheila grasps my hand tighter. "I'm sure you miss him baby," she says inching a little closer to me.

I smile at her happy she doesn't seem to want out of here. "Moretti Jr. has been looking for me and my brother ever since. That's why we go by your maiden name and our house and cars are registered under a fake business. I appreciate you for not questioning anything I've ever done, and you always were a great wife. Honestly, I couldn't have done this without you." I stare at her deeply, wanting to just pull her into my arms and kiss her as if I haven't seen her in years. "Basically, that's my life." I look at her, pleased that she's not going to leave me but shocked she's not angrier than she is. "How can you be so calm about everything I just told you," I question.

"I understand that everything you did was to protect us. I wish you would have trusted me enough to let me in. You never know what I could have done to help," she says straight-faced.

"Help? No offense babe but how would you be able to help? You were not raised from the streets like I was. You were that preppy girl with excellent grades and credit," I say skeptically.

"No offense taken. What makes you think that I didn't know how you were moving in the streets? Do you really think I would have moved abruptly in the middle of the night with no questions asked? Do you really think I wouldn't have questioned why we are using my maiden name and the fact that we are living the way we are financially? Do you think I'm that naïve?" She looks somewhat annoyed that I would think so little of her aptitude to understand the possibility of what I might be doing for us to live as we do. "Let me explain something to you husband. The last name that we're using is a name from someone who has been deceased for many years. Do you know who Thaddeus Blackman is?"

"Yes. Who don't know who he is? He is the most dangerous man of all time. Nobody fucks with him. I mean nobody."

"Well babes, Thaddeus Blackman is my father."

"What!" I hop up out of my seat. "You got to be kidding me. No way! *The* Thaddeus Blackman! I can't believe this. Seriously? Even Moretti fears him. Hell, everybody fears Thaddeus Blackman. My father-in-law is *The* Thaddeus Blackman," I pace the floor again as I somewhat gloat.

"Yes baby. That's my dad," she says as she looks at me and laughs. "He taught all of us how to protect ourselves, to always keep a low profile. Get a good education and keep your family secrets to yourself. If you wouldn't have told me about you and your family, I would have never told you about mine. My dad knows all about you and I would have never married you if he didn't approve."

I saunter over to her and sits beside her. "Your dad knows about me?"

"Of course he knows about you and we have protection because of it."

"I thought he was dead. How does he know about me? When and how do you communicate with him? Hell! You told me you your Dad left when you were a baby, and you don't remember him. You played your role very well. I would have never guessed that you are the daughter of the most notorious killer of all time."

"Yes, everyone thinks my father is dead, but he's alive and well. My dad carried himself with poise. No one would have ever guessed he is who he is. He's highly educated, and his looks are deceiving. He loves his family to death and just like you, no one knows we exist." She takes a deep breath. "I still can't tell you how I communicate with my father, just trust me, I must check in once a week to let him know everything is okay with us."

My mind immediately wonders off thinking of my father-in-law. Thaddeus has so many bodies under his belt that I've lost count. It seems as though the FBI could never pin any of the murders on him. I hope one day I can meet the infamous Thaddeus Blackman. However, now that I know who her father really is, I'm hoping she hasn't confided too much. He might want to shoot me.

"Okay honey. I understand clearly, are we going to tell the girls? I talked to my sister the other day and she told me the girls know that they have two uncles, but she's not sure how much the other kids told them. The boys may have told them everything, so she suggested that I talk to them before they come to us."

"I am not telling them about their grandfather. That approval has to come from my dad. I do not go against his wishes. It's bad enough that I told you who my dad is. I'm going to let him know that I told you, but it's a must that we do not tell the girls about him. If you are willing to tell them about you and your side of the family, I'm with you 100%."

"Yeah, I think it's time they know the truth, which they may already know. Did you realize how they were acting when they came back from Virginia? Zak didn't want to be around us. She probably wanted to say something as soon as she walked through the door."

"We will sit them down when they come home for the holidays. Do you really want to tell them then and ruin their holiday?" she asks.

"It's now or never. If they already know a little, it's best to tell them everything."

"Babe, how was it growing up with Thaddeus Blackman?" I ask excited to hear the details of someone I admired.

"My daddy raised us to get an education and carry ourselves with dignity. By the time I met you I was already a black belt in karate, excellent in boxing and I can handle a gun as easy as drinking a glass of water...and let's not forget I am an O.R. nurse. I will cut you up like you just had plastic surgery.

"I'm glad I never raised a hand to you," I say jokingly knowing I would never do that anyway.

"I'm glad you didn't either. I love you, but I would hurt you if you ever did," she says sincerely.

"By the way, what do you plan to do about Ms. Beatrice? Don't think I forgot about her ass. This thing you have with her has come to an end. I've given you too much freedom. It's time to put my foot down."

I stare at her knowing she means business and for some

reason, her sass has completely hardened my dick. However, her tone somehow makes me cower away from her.

"I understand you moved her here for her protection due to the fact that she's Q's mother, but any infidelities you're having with her ended those last three days you spent with her. I need you to make it clear to her that it's completely over. Q is a grown woman and there's no need for you to go over there for anything. Now, have I made myself clear?"

Fuck! I'm so horny now, but she's not going to let me lay one finger on her. "Yes honey. You made yourself crystal clear. I apologize for putting you through so much heartache and pain for so many years."

"You have a lot of making up to do. Please do not think that it's just that simple. We have a bigger problem on our hands with the Moretti family. For once and for all we need to let them know this family is not going to be in hiding anymore," she says continuing to let me know how things are going to go now.

"You are absolutely right babe. This man has had me and my brother in hiding for 8 years, I'm done. I didn't tell you I actually ran into Hector yesterday. He told me Moretti was using his baby sister's house to stash drugs and money. He believes his sister was skimming money from Moretti, so he had his baby sister killed. His sister had two kids. Hector believes his nephew either saw them kill his mom and or heard them kill his mom. His niece was a baby at the time, so he doesn't think she'll remember anything. Hector asked for my help to take Moretti down and I, of course, agreed."

"I'm all in. Don't think for a second you are not including me anymore.

Let's take the Moretti's down!"

CHAPTER 14

FAMILY SECRETS

ZAK

"Hey Q, are you finished packing so we can get on the road? I'm so excited to go home!" I ask.

"Yes, I'm almost done. Give me ten minutes. Did M and Irie leave?"

"No, not yet. They're outside packing up their cars."

Q and I pretend to take a long time packing so that M and Irie can head out before us. This is something we've always done just in case anyone decides to follow us to see where we live. Our upbringing has us a little paranoid at times, but we do what we gotta do. We say our goodbyes and told them we would see them soon, and then waited for an hour to pass before we left.

Q was the chauffeur for our drive home while I played our favorite songs. We sang along with every song, laughing and hiking on each other's voice. We got home in record time with Q being the driver. As soon as we walked through the door, our parents hugged us so tight as if we were away for years. The vibe in the house was definitely different. I couldn't put my finger on it, but I liked it. Once we unpack, we went Christmas shopping with mommy and Daddy's black card.

We had a lot of Christmas shopping to do considering all of

our cousins are coming up for the holidays. They will be here for Christmas and the New Year. I don't think my grandparents are coming. Grams is not ready to face daddy. After all these years, she still blames him for her other son getting killed. Aunt Jackie and all ten cousins are coming, luckily our house is large enough to accommodate everyone. We have six bedrooms in the house—One bedroom in the basement and a Murphy bed and two bedrooms in the guest house. Mom made sure she had plenty of everything for the family because this was her first-time meeting all of our cousins. Mommy says she only saw Aunt Jackie once—on the day of our senior graduation.

As I begin down the stairs I overhear my parents talking, so I stopped at the top of the stairs and eavesdrop.

"I'm so excited to finally meet your family. It's good the girls have family they can be around. I hate how we kept them so secluded growing up. I hope they understand and forgive us." Mom says to daddy as she fluffs the pillows on the couch for the hundredth time.

"I believe they will understand. Our daughters are intelligent, mature young ladies. They will finally see the truth about who their dad really is." Daddy says nervously.

"Hey, Jamar just text me and says they are pulling up to the house now," I say as I run down the stairs interrupting my parents conversation.

Q follows right behind me to meet them outside.

As we all stood in the driveway, two big black Suburban trucks with tinted windows pull up to the house. The twins were the first to hop out of the truck, running top speed towards us. Tristan jumps in Q's arms as Trinity jumps in my arms. We both gave them a kiss on the cheek and spun them around before we put them down. We were so excited to see our family, we hugged each one as they exited the truck.

We began introducing everyone to my Mom, who immediately fell in love with the twins. They are only eight and mom hasn't been around a little kid in years. Daddy and Auntie Jackie hugged each other so long we all felt their missed family connection as she wept in my father's arms. Their embrace was so intense that Q came to my side and squeezed my hand, knowing I would be crying myself in a second. It was a happy moment.

"I was hoping mom and dad would be here," my father says to Aunt Jackie with sadness in his voice.

"She's still not ready brother, just give her a little more time." Aunt Jackie says trying to console daddy.

We all longed to see that kind of embrace between my daddy and his mother also. My parents rushed them in the house because my mother had prepared a hot feast for the family to enjoy upon their arrival. It was pretty much a smorgasbord because she didn't know what anyone liked. She couldn't just make fried chicken, she had to bake it too. There was also barbecue beef ribs, mac and cheese, collard greens, yams, and potato salad. She even thought to make chicken nuggets and fries just in case the twins didn't eat what she prepared.

At the sight of the food, my cousins agreed they would get the luggage out of the trucks later. We all sat down together as a family should for Sunday dinner. Something I hope would happen many times. It was great to see everyone laughing and joking about things my father missed over the years. My mother was just listening in trying to grasp the family dynamics, clearly enjoying their company. For me, it was good to know I have such an extensive, protective family. Something my daddy should have never kept from us. I do understand for the most part why. I just wish he would come out and say it.

Once dinner was over, my dad and the older male cousins retrieved the luggage from the trucks and then decide to go downstairs to my daddy's man cave. I'm pretty sure it was to catch up on the street life. A life my daddy has tried very hard to keep a secret and something I feel he might miss for some reason. After all, it's what he knows...what he grew up doing according to our cousins...and it seems that it was a life he had to give up forcefully in the dead of night. After my mother and aunt finished cleaning the kitchen, they get the twins ready for bed. Mom didn't want the twins to hear adult conversations.

"Come on y'all. Let's go downstairs with the men and see what they are doing," Mom says to all of us females.

When we get down there, I see Mom give Daddy a head nod and then walks over to sit next to him. Mom grabs daddy's hand and says, "it's ok babe."

"I have something to tell you all," my daddy says suddenly. He stares in my and Q's direction and drops his head suddenly. A move that makes me think he's ashamed at whatever he's about to say. If only he knew he could tell us anything and trust us with it. We have never spoken of anything we weren't supposed to and would never give him a reason to doubt us. I'm not sure why he thinks he needs to keep holding things back. We're both grown women now.

Daddy begins to stutter the more he realizes that what he considers is a bombshell to his little girls is about to explode from his own words. "Girls—I-I don't want you to feel...feel a certain way," he clears his throat, "way about what I'm - I'm about to say but—."

"Oh my god! Daddy just tell us everything about you being a drug dealer," Q interjects.

Everyone explodes obnoxiously into laughter, easing the tension in the room, and more important, my daddy's nerves. The laughing was so infectious, even my daddy joined in with a boisterous laugh I hadn't heard in years. It's obvious my daddy didn't want to tell us because he thought for some reason we would look at him different. Which is just ridiculous.

"Okay girls," my daddy continued once he caught his breath

from laughing so hard. "I grew up in Newark, and my dad was best friends with a man name Francesco Moretti Sr."

I look over at Q praying to myself that daddy didn't just say the name Moretti.

"Your grandaddy was one of Moretti Sr.'s right-hand men in the drug game. As years went on, they decided to teach their sons the drug game. Which would be Moretti Jr., me and your two uncles, James and Phil."

As I refocus my mind from what I pray is not happening, my heart begins to beat heavily against my chest as I hear Moretti's name again. This can't be. There's no way the world can be that small. I can't believe that the man I've been fuckin' is a friend of my father and his brothers. Q grabs my hand and squeezes it tightly, clearly thinking what I am. There's just no fuckin' way.

"Well, one night we were to do a job for Moretti. The job was to kill someone that Moretti says was selling drugs in one of his areas. My brother Phil was tired of being Moretti's flunky. He decided not to do the job and he went back to Moretti's house without me and James." My daddy becomes uncomfortable at the mention of Phil going to that house alone. This must be where shit hits the fan.

"He told Moretti he wasn't doing the job and Phil knew the consequences of that, he thought he would be safe. I guess he felt that way since he was engaged to Moretti's oldest daughter and she was pregnant with his twins. Sadly that wasn't the case. Moretti made his 13-year-old daughter shoot and kill my brother."

Q squeezes my hand much tighter this time, digging her nails into my flesh but that doesn't seem to calm me. Not one bit. All I wanted to do was run away from this conversation. Freeze time and try to go back to before I had given into Moretti's advances.

"Phil must have known this was going to happen, because

he took 2.5 million dollars from Moretti, stashing it in our safe house for me and James to find. We decide to split it three ways, giving Phil's to my father.

Everyone was quiet as if listening to a horror story. Especially Q and I. My heart is beating heavily like it's the only sound in the room and I'm hoping no one can feel my anxiety building in the room.

"That same night, James went underground, and I moved us out here to this house. To this day, Moretti has a hit out on me and my brother James," my daddy finally finishes.

"Oh my god! Oh my god! Oh my god!" Q and I say in unison.

"Well, y'all can't talk at the same time. What is it?" Mom questions.

"Okay Zak you tell 'em, cause I think I'm in shock," Q says shaking her head.

"Okay let me get my mind right. You know our friend from school, who we now share a house with?" I stare at the others who are silent as they nod their heads. "Well, her name is Maria Moretti." I pause, but decide not to look up at them, instead I continue on to say the worst of it. "She told us a story about her dad making her kill a guy because he didn't do what he was told. Her dad told her she has to be a boss . . . Oh my god, I'm shaking."

"M killed our Uncle?" Q says in disbelief, as she held up her head.

"Your friend killed my father?" Trent yelled as he stood angrily. "Where is this bitch? I'm gonna shoot that bitch in her fuckin' head."

"No worries nephew. We are going to get all their asses," Daddy assures Trent.

"Wait a minute babe. When you said his name the other day, I kept saying to myself that name sounds so familiar. He came to the hospital a couple of weeks ago. He has a bad heart.

He was flirting and asked me to be his visiting home nurse. I have his number and his address. I'm supposed to call him and let him know if I would accept the job," Mom explains.

"Okay Auntie, you can be our way in to get to this mother fucker. I'm so sorry. Excuse my mouth but I'm mad right now," Trent says retaking his seat.

"No problem sweetie. I understand," Mom says to Trent in a sincere tone.

"Nah Sheila! I can't put you at risk like that. That man is heartless, and he will kill you or have you killed in the blink of an eye," Daddy exclaims, slightly raising his voice.

"He doesn't know my real identity. All he knows is I'm a nurse and he wants me to become his visiting home nurse." Mom tries reassuring Daddy, but I don't think it's working.

"I can take a family leave from my job. I will have to move into the town house we have, just in case he has some of his men follow me when I leave his home," Mom says as if she has already devised a plan.

"Oh, you got this all figured out huh?" Daddy says sternly.

"Babe, I got this. Our townhouse has a safe room, and you have guns throughout the house, so I'll have some protection. We are no longer living in hiding. Our girls are literally friends with and living with the enemy." Mom says knowing that mentioning us will get his blood boiling. "What if he found out who they really are and did something to them?" Mom continued just to make her point.

"Sheila, are you trying to piss me off to get your way?" My daddy snaps.

All I can think about is me having sex with the man who had my uncle killed and put my family into hiding for years. I can't possibly reveal this to them. They will lose their shit, and I can't have that happen. Not now, and probably not ever. I glance over at Q who is shooting me that what-the-fuck-you-going-to-do look. I know our connection has her feeling my anxiety. I literally slept with the enemy. I know Q is ready to say *I told you so,* but that isn't something I want to hear right now. We both knew there would be consequences for having this relationship with Moretti. Who knew that consequence would stretch beyond Maria.

"Why are you girls so quiet? I know this has to be a lot for you. I don't want you to stay with them and y'all are going to have to take a break from school," Mom says.

"If I take a break that will affect my basketball scholarship," Q says staring at our dad.

"You know how we feel about school, but your life is more important to us than anything in this world. If Moretti finds out that you two are my daughter's, there's no telling what he will do to you. I will kill everybody and their momma if he hurts one of you," Daddy suddenly yells as he stands to pace the floor.

Jamar and Trent walk over to Daddy, trying to douse the flames of his impending explosion.

"Zak are you sure you're okay?" Mom asks peering at me.

There's no real way to lie to her. My mom knows me very well. She can probably sense by the look on my face that there's more to it than what I'm telling them.

"Yes Mom, I'm just sitting here thinking that my whole life is about to change if I have to stop going to school. Not to mention finding out my friend killed my uncle."

"Cuddy, you can go back to school as soon as we get rid of the Moretti family. Which means we gon' have to take out the whole family," Jamar explains.

"Yo!" Q suddenly shouts. "One night we went to a dinner party at their house. Zak asked the oldest daughter Gabbie if she had a boyfriend or was she planning to get married or something like that. She looked at M like she wanted to kill her. Now we know why. Her dad had her little sister kill her Fiancé-baby daddy. Oh wait, she was pregnant with twins. The twins?

Our cousins are her kids? M's niece and nephew. Oh! This is some shit." Everything begins to come together in her head as she speaks excitedly. "Sorry y'all," Q apologized for her foul language in front of her parents.

"No wonder they looked mixed. They are. Trinity looks like her mom and M with their jet-black long hair," Q continues.

"It's not Gabbie's fault. We got to save her from them. She never met her kids," Q says remembering the story Destiny told them when they were visiting in Virginia.

"You all better make it clear who's who, 'cause I'm blasting everybody,"

Trent says as he walked back over to where we're sitting.

"Let me see how we can put this shit together cause we have to end this once and for all. We'll talk about this some more tomorrow," Daddy says.

CHAPTER 15

SMALL WORLD

ZAK

I can't believe I've been sleeping with Moretti for months now. No way I can let my family know this. My daddy would have a heart attack if he finds out his baby girl is sleeping with his enemy. This is so fucked up on so many levels. Of all the people in the world, we befriend the one person who killed my uncle. Just then a message from Moretti comes through asking when he can see me again. I choose to avoid it for now. I have to.

Q interrupts my thoughts letting me know Irie called her and invited all of us to her family's pre-Christmas celebration. Q reminds her that our family is visiting and there will be ten of us coming to the party. Irie didn't skip a beat because she's in the partying mood. We decide to accept the invitation and go to Irie's later that night. After the night we just had, I was ready to go turn up Jamaican style. I know it's gonna be lit. We all need to get our minds off the shit we just found out about our family.

"What are we going to do if M is at the party?' I asked Q.

"I don't know, cause we are not going to be able to hold Trent back if he sees her." Q responds.

"Well since he doesn't know what she looks like we can tell him she's not here." I say.

"Let's see how that works, okay let's finish getting ready before they wonder what's taking us so long," Q states.

We all got dressed and ready for Irie's family party. I have to say, we are a good-looking family. We leave our home rolling deep as usual. All ten of us got into Jamar and Trent's trucks, I am immediately happy that neither Q nor I had to do the driving.

It doesn't take us long to get to Irie's aunt and uncle's house. It was extremely gorgeous, decorated beautifully with Christmas lights with a little snow on the grounds. The reflection of the Christmas lights on the snow made it look stunning.

Once we get inside, shockingly there were only us there. This better not be some fucking setup. My mind immediately goes to the worst, considering what my daddy reveals.

"Where is everyone? I thought the party was here," I question Irie instead of jumping to conclusions.

"No, I'm sorry. The party is at a hall they rented for the event. My family has a tradition that we meet up here first and do a toast off before we leave. I wanted to invite you to our home because you've never been here," Irie explains.

At first my cousins were leery, and they noticeably put their hands in their pockets.

They stay ready, so they don't have to get ready.

Irie then introduces us all to her Aunt and Uncle and they gave us all welcoming hugs and hellos.

Suddenly, Jamar spots three dudes coming from upstairs. "Oh shit. What are y'all doing here?"

"Wow! You know them? Those are my cousins, Winston, Donavan and Clive from Virginia. This is a small world," Irie says smiling, pleased that everyone was familiar with one another.

"I didn't think to ask Zak and Q if y'all knew them," Irie says.

"Oh, it's about to be lit! lit! These are our boys, they like fam.

You know we were about to pull out the strap. We thought this was a set up at first," Jamar says as if that's a normal response as they all slap five and give each other a manly hug.

"Yo fam! What's good homies? Who you'll know here?" Donovan asked.

"Apparently our cousins have been friends all this time and go to school together," Jamar admits.

"Damn. This is a small world. It's on and poppin'! Let's go turn the fuck up. You'll already know how we party. They ain't ready fam. "Cum wi guh party!,"

Winston yells out. Irie's aunt taps on her glass to get our attention and then her aunt and uncle make a toast, and then we were off to celebrate.

As we walk out as a group, I notice Donovan hold Irie back in the foyer. The conversation seems intense, until I see tears fall from Irie's eyes. I know the only time she has cried was when she told us about her childhood. I'll have to ask Q to talk to her, make sure she's all right.

Donovan follows a smiling Irie out of the house to get in the car, so that we can follow them to the hall they rented.

We arrive at the hall, I see instantly what Irie was talking about. People seemed to be partying even on the outside, dancing, drinking, and smoking as if they didn't have a care in the world. Once we get inside, the music bumped so loud I felt it in my chest, and I couldn't wait to get on the dance floor. That's exactly what I did...until my feet were sore, this party is lit, but I needed a break. Besides, no matter how hard I tried that looming Moretti problem resided at the back of my mind.

"Damn her cousins look good. They look like Kofi Siriboe from that movie Girl's Trip. I'm definitely getting with one of them," Q says as I pull her off the dance floor.

"Yes, they are good looking but I have a serious situation on my hands," I remind my sister.

"Yes you do. What are you going to do about your secret lover?" Q questioned seriously.

"I don't know Q. You know this shit got me all the way fucked up. It's been on my mind ever since we found out. Can you believe I've been sleeping with the man that had his daughter, who is our friend, kill our uncle? This shit is killing me. I had to be on some, *be blocked or be blessed* shit, because he's been calling my phone every day," I say saddened. I can't even lie at this point. The man was somewhat growing on me.

"Yeah sissy they are going to kill your secret lover," Q says again as they both shared a laugh.

"I can't wait to see what the plan is," I say to Q.

"Me either," Q agreed. "I think you want them to kill him, so your ass don't have to deal with the repercussions." Q stares at me, silently awaiting my response.

My sister knows me all so well. If they don't kill his ass I will have to. I will have to find a way to only look at him, as the man who put a guy's life in an innocent's child's hand to kill my uncle.

"Silence is golden, but on another note, don't you think we should forgive Irie? I didn't know our cousins were so close" Q questioned abandoning her initial line of questioning.

"If Irie is good and watches her mouth, I'm good. Oh yeah and I saw her and her cousin Donovan talking before we left, and she was crying at first, make sure to ask Irie what was wrong." I tell Q.

"Yeah I saw that too, I'm definitely going to ask what happened." Q says.

Before we could finish our conversation, Irie walks up to Q and me. "Zak I want to put whatever beef we got behind us, because our families are too close for us to be beefing. I love you and I'm sorry."

I accepted her apology because she seemed sincere, this

time. We hugged and just like that, we were cool again. No hard feelings. Our cousins wouldn't have it any other way.

"I have a confession to make," Irie admits to Q and I.

"What the fuck! We just made up and you want to confess some shit," Q says as they laugh.

"Nah nothing like that. Remember the incident at the club?"

Q gave Irie a look as to say, bitch don't make me punch the shit out of you again.

"Chill Q. I've been sleeping with Kareem ever since I was a senior in high school."

Q and I look at each other, "Are you fuckin' serious," we say in unison.

"No wonder his ass was quiet sitting in VIP. He got drunk and didn't say a word for the rest of the night," Q reminded us.

"That's why I said it's a long story and I don't want to end our dysfunctional relationship because I love him."

Q and I just stare at each other, because I'm in a more dysfunctional situation than she is. I sure can't give her any advice.

"It's fine, I'll figure it out. I wanted to let you know because I know you all know them.

"Chile, I need a drink after listening to y'all entanglements." Q says.

I shot a *look to kill* at my sister. She knew to shut her mouth.

I nudged Q so she can ask Irie about her the conversation she had with her cousin Donovan before we left for the party.

"Irie I'm not trying to be nosey or anything, but we saw you and your cousin Donovan talking just before we left, and you were crying. Is everything ok?" Q tries to sound sincere and not nosey.

"Yeah everything is fine now. That bum ass mother-fuckathat violated me when I were a kid, they handled that shit." Irie says and paused to look at our reaction.

"His body parts are floating around in different places." Irie continues.

The tears run down Irie's face again as she tells us what her cousin shared with her. They were tears of relief and a mixture of joy. We hugged her tight to assure her that they we share her sentiments.

Irie wipes her tears as she looks up at us and whispers, "your cousins helped my cousins get rid of his body."

"Damn that's some deep shit." Q states.

At that moment we realized how close our cousins really were.

"He's no longer alive to hurt anyone else!" Irie exclaims.

We high fived each other with big smiles on our faces.

"Irie, I didn't see M here tonight, where is she?' I ask.

"Oh you know how her dad is, he's also having a Pre-Christmas celebration so she couldn't make it." Irie responds.

I'm so glad M is not here cause I don't know what would have happened.

"Yeah her dad has parties for every occasion." Q interjects once she realizes I'm in my thoughts.

"Let's get back on the dance floor before my aunt and uncle think you're not enjoying their party," Irie says as she sashays back to the dance floor.

Irie's family is so nice and party harder than we do. We were having a great time, considering the family secrets we've learned.

Before we know it, the host at the hall has to flick the lights off and on to signal that the party was now over. We take the time to thank Irie's aunt and uncle for inviting us, before heading back to our house completely exhausted...from the partying and my racing thoughts.

As soon as I my head hits the pillow, I see the glow of my phone in the darkness. I of course think to ignore it and check it right away, but with the plan ready to be set in motion, I clumsily reach over to grab the phone. My eyes widen at the sight of Moretti contacting me yet again. My stomach hits the goddamn floor like I just ate a fucking brick.

Moretti: You think you can just avoid me?

I don't respond, instead stare at the message unsure of what I should be saying. Fear comes over me, not so much because he can have me killed at any moment...by his daughter while I slept even. The problem is more my family.

Moretti: You've already given yourself to me. You're mine. I will have my tongue in my pussy whenever I choose to. That time will come.

Fuck my life.

CHAPTER 16

MYSTERY MAN WITH SUNNI

SHEILA

The first thing on my mind when I open my eyes is going to the Moretti house. Although I'm trying to be brave for my family and keep the girls safe, I know that family will not hesitate to harm me in some way if they learn my true identity somehow. If anything should happen to me, I know my husband will never forgive himself and I will leave my daughters in the hands of his mistress...who's no mother figure. I have to be sure to play it safe. Pay attention to what's happening and get the intel the family needs to exact their revenge as they see fit. It's what my father has taught me to do. Although, he would probably be the first one to want to put a bullet in Tony's head, I know I'll have to ease my husband's mind.

"Good morning honey," my husband rolls over interrupting my mental rampage. "I feel like this needs to be said again. You know I couldn't sleep last night because I'm not comfortable with you going to work for Moretti. He will have you killed, or he won't let you leave. He will torture you if he finds out who you are." He squeezes me harder to bring me closer to him as if I could be any closer. "I thought about this all night too. What do you think your father would say? He would kill me, literally, if he knew I would allow you to do something like this," he says desperately trying to convince me not to go to work for Moretti.

"Babes, I understand your concern, but for one, I will do whatever I have to, to keep my family safe. My father has prepared me for things like this. I don't know if my dad would agree, but I know he would understand."

He gives me the side eye as he gets out of bed.

"I'm going to talk to my dad tomorrow and I will let him know. Trust me, he'll figure out what's the best way to handle this. Everything will be fine," she says sitting up on the bed. "I'm going downstairs to make breakfast and then start dinner, it's Christmas Eve. We will put everything in motion after the new year," I say hoping the mere mention of my father will help ease his doubt.

After I made breakfast, I called everyone to the dinning room to eat. We all sit for breakfast, enjoying each other's company. I couldn't help but stare at my preoccupied daughter who has been preoccupied with something. Something that has been silencing her far too much and I need to find out what that is. No matter how many times I ask her if she's okay, she just withholds the truth as if she doesn't know I can see right through her lies. She shoots me a smile no doubt trying to let me know she's good once again, but I know she's not.

"Uncle Tony, we decided we are going to stay up here until this situation with the Moretti family is dealt with. We are in this together. After the holidays we can send Aunt Jackie back home with the twins so we can handle this once and for all," Jamar says. He looks around the table as the cousins nod in agreement. "This family cannot allow someone else to keep us in hiding. Especially to the point that we haven't seen our dad in eight years. I thought he was just a dead beat, now I know the truth. It's way too many secrets in this family. We gotta get it together. I understand keeping secrets from everyone else but at least we can tell each other what's going on." Jamar continues.

"I appreciate all of you. I'm glad that we are finally going to handle this shit," Tony says as he gets up from the dining table.

"Unc, I'm not gon' lie, I thought you had something to do with Uncle Phil getting killed. For years no one knew what happened to him, and Grams wouldn't talk to you or didn't want to accept anything from you." Chelsea tries to explain to my husband, trying to sound less cruel than her statement demonstrates.

Tony stands in front of his dining room chair, with his elbow leaning on the tall back of it. He erects his body as soon as the words leave Chelsea's mouth. From his movements, we all thought he was going to be upset but he wasn't.

"I'm glad you're being honest Chelsea and I can see how that would make everyone think I was involved, but I promise you, I would never do anything to hurt my brother or anyone in my family," Tony says with pure conviction as he walked back in forth in the dining room.

"Don't worry. I'm gonna fix this," Tony adds.

Christmas Day
Zak

The twins awaken everyone before the sun comes up. They were so excited to see so many gifts under the tree. Tristan was so thrilled when he opened his PS5 that he stops opening his other gifts. Mom and daddy bought so many gifts. I think they were more excited than the twins. I know it was probably because this was the first time we ever had family, or anyone for that matter, over to our house.

Trinity's favorite gifts were her LOL Dolls, but everyone

enjoyed their gifts. We stayed up talking, eating and drinking eggnog in our matching black and red-checkered pajamas, that mom insisted everyone wear so we could take family pictures.

Mom and Aunt Jackie seemed to have become best of friends almost immediately. It's good seeing her smile, which we haven't seen in so long. Mom and Daddy seem to be in love again. I guess they thought we didn't see the change, but whatever. I'm glad they are happy with each other now.

The doorbell rings and everyone was on guard. Especially once Daddy mentions that no one ever comes to the house.

"I don't know who the hell it can be," he announces.

He treads heavily over to the front door and swings it open. The cousins stare at the person in shock, as Q and me wonder who he is. There stood this tall, gorgeous man in a full Sunni and low haircut. Destiny runs over to the mysterious man and yells, "Daddy is that really you?"

"Yes, it's me baby girl," Uncle James says as he lifts Destiny off of her feet hugging her tightly as if she was a little girl.

Daddy was still in shock, but was able to tell his brother to come inside. Everyone had so many questions for Uncle James, and for the first time in my life, I saw Daddy shed a tear. The entire house was in an unbelievable uproar. We all burst into tears as we pulled him into the living room to sit with us. The twins just looked at us wondering whom this strange man could be. My mom, Q, the twins and I have never laid eyes on Uncle James before. Daddy walks Uncle James over to mom and introduces them. When daddy introduces him to the twins, he stands there in shock to see his brother Phil's kids there with the family. He hugged them so tight they both yelled, "I can't breathe." Everyone laughed and Uncle James let them go. He then embraced his sons, and nobody wanted to let go. They held on to one another for dear life.

"I thought you were dead," Jamil says as the tears flow once again.

We all sat down in the family room and the twins continued playing with their toys. Aunt Jackie couldn't believe her eyes as she kept saying aloud, '*my brother is really here*'.

"I know I have a lot of explaining to do. I want to start off by telling my kids I apologize for staying away for so long, but I had my reasons. I've always watched you guys to make sure you were all right." He pauses a moment and then faces my father as his expression turns serious. "I was watching you too brother. I saw you talking to Hector at the gas station. After the third time you met with him, I noticed a car following you. He followed you around town and I saw that it was one of Moretti's dudes. I don't know if Hector is a snitch, but it was definitely one of Moretti's dudes following you."

You can see a glimmer of fear come over my father, but he quickly suppresses it, not wanting any of us to worry. Clearly his cover was blown, and he had no idea. "Nah, not Hector," Daddy says while shaking his head.

"You don't have to worry about him, Moretti's dude, 'cause I killed his ass. He followed you home the other day and was posted up across the street watching your house. I don't think he had a chance to tell Moretti where you live," Uncle James reassured everyone.

"How do you know for sure?" Daddy asked.

"I made his ass take the password off his phone before I killed him," Uncle James says coldly.

"My brother is back and in effect," Daddy boasts.

"I don't think Hector would set me up though. Moretti had his sister killed and he wants to get Moretti too. So why would he tell Moretti about me?" Daddy asks.

"Uncle Tony, I don't trust none of them. What if he told Hector he would kill his other family members and Hector gave you up?" Machai pitches his concerns.

"That's a valid point nephew, but I trust Hector and I don't think he gave me up. To be on the safe side, we have to put this thing in motion quick because I don't know if Moretti's dude told him where I live."

We played catch up with my Uncle James. The men of the family were anxious, so they all went to the basement to discuss how to handle taking down Moretti.

By the time New Year's Eve rolled around we were so worked up that my father asked everyone to stay home and celebrate. So we did.

Mom and Aunt Jackie cooked, and we partied and waited to watch the ball drop, the twins fell asleep way before the ball dropped.

CHAPTER 17

INFILTRATION

SHEILA

Aunt Jackie and the twins head back home to Virginia as planned, while the rest of the family stayed to ensure the plan is executed without a hitch. A plan that involves me doing everything right. I try not to be concerned about everything falling on my shoulders, but I demanded that I be part of the decision-making and my husband has complied. Can't go back on things now. I head downstairs to where my husband and his nephews are talking.

"Uncle Tony, we got our boy driving up here to bring us some heat. He's bringing Glocks, AK47s, Nines, 38s and hand grenades . . . all that shit," Jamar informed Tony.

"How is he going to get all of that up here from Virginia?" Tony questions.

"We got this Unc. He's going to rent a U-Haul truck and put a whole house full of furniture in it. He's going to hide the weapons inside the furniture," Jamar explained.

"Okay nephew. You'll got it mapped out huh?" Tony seems impressed.

"Yeah Unc. My family will no longer be in hiding if we have anything to do with it," Trent joins the conversation.

"I'm going to take a leave of absence from work and I will

call Moretti and ask him if the job is still available. That will be our way inside," I add once I make it into the living room.

My husband stares at me no doubt still concerned about my involvement. "Okay. We will continue this meeting tomorrow after I talk to my dear wife tonight, because I still have reservations about her doing this. If anything happens to her, I'm killing e'rybody," Tony says as he begins to walk me back upstairs.

"I understand Unc. We are going to handle it however you see fit, but I believe that Auntie is our best way in. It don't get no better than that," Machai says.

"She's not going to just walk in and kill him. She's going to go in, be his nurse and get him to trust her. It may take a minute, but we got time. We never rush a job," Kyle adds.

"I hear you, but we will discuss this further tomorrow," Tony responds.

As I follow my husband upstairs, I hear James whispers.

"I understand where Tony is coming from, I'm not sure if sending his wife in Moretti's house is a good idea. That man is the devil himself. You don't know him like we know him."

His statement rings true considering my husband's reluctance. There's just no other real choice in the matter. I have to do this.

"Listen hun, I know you want to do your part to help the family, but I'm not sure if going inside his house is the best solution," my husband says, concern gleaming from his dark brown eyes.

"I know you have concerns honey, but I talked to my dad the other day and he said he'll keep an eye out for me while I'm there. I don't know how he's going to do it, but I trust him, and you should too." I say hoping those words will ease his worry. He stares at me wanting to believe that my father will not let anything happen, but I don't think that's good enough for him. Not now anyway. "I'm only going to be working there three days out of the week, and I'll stay at our townhouse just in case he has someone follow me. I don't want him to get a heads up on you and the girls."

He takes a deep breath and crosses his arms at his chest. He doesn't say anything at first, as if he's finally accepting what's going to happen. "Okay honey, I'm agreeing on one condition. It's a must that you call and let me know you're okay. I need check-ins as much as possible."

Seems a bit risky, but I'm sure I'll come up with a way for that to happen. I walk over to him and cup his cheek, making his shoulders visibly relax. "Okay," I say simply.

The next day I call Mr. Moretti and ask if he still needs a nurse. He seems genuinely pleased to hear from me, and instantly hires me to be his nurse for three days a week after minimal negotiation. We agree that I would start that following Monday.

—————————————————————————

My first day at the Moretti's house, my nerves were all over the place just thinking of the evil that Moretti has done. I know this is something that needs to be done, so I push those inner feelings to the side to do what I had come to do.

As I was given a tour around the huge, gorgeous home his employee informed me there were cameras throughout the outside of the house but none within. Mrs. Moretti didn't want cameras inside of her home. His employee took me to the study to sit down with Moretti and go over his expectations from me. He further informs me that I will be paid every Friday in cash and asked if that was a problem. Of course I agree considering I don't give a shit about taking his money, and then we walk out to meet his daughter and wife.

There were about six of his other employees that I was

allowed to explain his condition in front of them. One of the men gave me a wink and a head nod. I don't know what that was about, but I continue. I go into further detail concerning the medical terms with the family so everyone can be on board with his condition. However, Gabbie seems completely uninterested as though she didn't care and excuses herself. I also tell them that a heart monitor will be delivered here today or tomorrow and explain to Moretti the importance of being on the monitor. I further insist on preparing meals for him because eating properly is a main factor.

The monitor was delivered the next day, which was actually sent over by my father, there was a camera installed inside of it so he could keep an eye on me. He told me that he would only be able to see me in whichever room the monitor is placed. So, I put it in Mr. and Mrs. Moretti's bedroom. While Moretti slept the monitor would be on.

As time went on Mr. Moretti seem to become comfortable with me. For some reason, Mrs. Moretti had a close watch over me. She asked me so many questions. Questions like, how her husband and I met, how long have I been a nurse, do I have children, where am I from? I thought she was a damn detective or something. She asked so many questions. At that point I realize I need to be extra cautious around her. I let her know that I was the only child, both my parents are deceased, I never married and had no children. It's just me.

On this particular day I arrived at the Moretti's home a little earlier to get my day started. As I head up the stairs to check on my patient I overhear, Mr. and Mrs. Moretti conversing. I stepped down a few stairs not to be seen but still in earshot of their conversation.

"Honey what's wrong with you? You haven't been acting like yourself for about a week or two now." Mrs. Moretti asks her husband.

"Something is not right. Hector has been acting strange

lately, so I put one of my men on him and now I haven't seen or heard from Dino in 2 weeks.

I didn't hear Mrs. Moretti respond, so Mr. Moretti continues to talk.

"He's not answering my calls and we can't locate his car or anything. I had two missed calls from him, but he didn't leave a message, so I'm not sure what's going on. Whatever it is, I believe Hector has something to do with it," Moretti insinuates.

"Honey you're just being paranoid. Hector has been working for you since he was 16 years old and he never crossed you. Why do you think he would do so now?" Mrs. Moretti asks. "I need you to calm down before you have another heart attack. You can send you're men out to look for Dino tomorrow."

As Mrs. Moretti walked out of her bedroom she notices Gabbie coming from hers.

"Gabbie, what are you doing up so early?" Mrs. Moretti asked her daughter.

"Mother! If you don't mind I'm going to the kitchen to fix myself some breakfast."

"Gabbie! I've had enough of you and your mood swings. Get your act together—."

"Or what mother? You and father will have me committed again? Or put me in the secret hiding place again? I'm so sick of you all running my life. Leave me alone!" Gabbie yells as I hear her stomp away.

"This discussion is not over Gabbie. We will finish this later," Mrs. Moretti says.

I start to walk up the stairs and pretended to cough so to be heard coming.

"It's over as far as I'm concerned," Gabbie snaps back as she walks down the stairs pass me. I utter good morning, but no one says anything.

I go into the bedroom to check on my patient and inform

him that I'll be back shortly with his breakfast and meds. During which, Mrs. Moretti stares at me coldly, probably assuming I overheard her and Gabbie's conversation.

As I go downstairs to prepare breakfast for my patient, Gabbie is eating a bowl of cereal. I ask if she was okay, to which she responds simply by saying fine. I didn't pressure her because I have a feeling we will talk later when her mom is out of the house. I take the breakfast and meds upstairs to Moretti, and not long after, Mrs. Moretti says she has errands to run before leaving for the day.

Once I'm done taking Mr. Moretti's vitals and giving him his meds, I go back to the kitchen to talk to Gabbie. The only place where plenty of our conversations have taken place, as I prepared meals for her dad. I've been here for two months now and Gabbie has confided in me about everything. I asked Gabbie if she's feeling well today, and she just breaks down and asks if she can trust me. So I reassure her that she can, because this is the perfect day to converse considering her mom was out running errands.

Gabbie explains that her parents had her committed to the psych ward, and she was diagnosed with having bipolar disorder. She also told me that she had a set of twins that were being raised by their other grandparents and she never saw them. Her parents made the doctors take them away as soon as she delivered them, and blamed it on her bipolar disorder. They claimed her condition wouldn't allow her to care for them as they would need to be. I asked Gabbie how her parents were able to admit her in the psych ward?

She stares through me with sad, lonely eyes compelling me to want to help her in any way possible. "Before I say anything else, I really need your word Nurse Monroe that I can truly trust you," Gabbie said with a look of desperation.

"Gabbie, you have my absolute word that you can trust me," I tell her.

"When I was eight months pregnant with twins, my dad had my fiancé killed because he didn't approve of us being together. He used to work for my father and one night my fiancé was tired of being ordered around by my dad. He stood up for himself, and my father doesn't like anyone to talk back or disobey him."

I sat listening intently, wanting her to tell me everything, so I made sure to not interrupt her.

"That night he told my 13-year-old sister to shoot my fiancé in the head. She did it— she killed him. Sadness fell over Gabbie and tears begin to flow down her face, so I stood to console her. She held up her hand, letting me know she was okay and continued. "That's when I had a breakdown. I'm not bipolar, but yes, I was depressed. How would you feel if your father had your little sister kill your fiancé and the father of your kids?" Gabbie asked harshly, making me nod assuring her. "The pills my parents make me take have me sleeping all day. Even when I was awake, I would feel extremely tired. I stopped taking them and my mind is much clearer now. They think I'm still taking them so whenever I'm around them I just act dazed, as if I'm still taking the pills," Gabbie explains.

I grab her hand and squeeze it letting her know I understand why she's behaving as she is. She must feel alone in this house, trapped even. I'm not sure how I can help her any sooner than the plan allows, but I know she will be happy to see her beautiful kids. Just by me knowing they were only a couple hours away from her, makes me feel for her. There's no way I can even be standing if someone took Zak from my arms when I had her.

"I really don't like any of my family. They have completely ruined my life. I was an accountant, doing very well for myself and I was about to get married. My sister acts like nothing ever happened. She's in college to become an attorney and they are drugging me with pills. It's okay though, I'm going to get all of them for what they did to me and my family." Gabbie blurts out.

"One thing at a time Gabbie. I know you want to get them back for what they did to you, but we have to make sure you are well after taking those pills for so long." Nurse Monroe instructs.

"I'm back to feeling like myself again. I stopped taking them shits a long time ago. My mind is no longer cloudy. They keep trying to make me feel like I'm crazy" Gabbie insists.

"They're trying to put the blame on me because Daddy told me not to get involved with a black man. Who cares about color? We were in love. I will get all three of them— Daddy, Mommy, and my dear Princess *Sister,*" Gabbie continues angrily.

"Gabbie, I'm sorry to hear all that has happened to you, and especially from your own family. I'm here if you ever need me for anything. Also, I'm going to help you with your medication. You can't just stop cold turkey. Go and bring me your pills so I can help you wean off of them," I offer. She quickly follows my instructions, I explained to Gabbie how to take her meds, but I also sneakily took some to crush in Mr. Moretti's food and drinks.

As time went on Gabbie and I became closer and closer. Of course, we didn't allow her Mom to see it though. I kept Mr. Moretti drugged up, so he rarely got out of bed. Mrs. Moretti asked why he sleeps so much, and I said it's due to his condition, but all of his vitals are great, and there was no need to worry. I noticed that Mrs. Moretti would remain out of the house much more due to Mr. Moretti staying in bed majority of the day. That gave me and Gabbie a lot of time together.

It wasn't until days later that Gabbie approaches me with something so unexpected that it almost knocked me off of my feet.

"Hi Nurse Monroe. How are you today?" Gabbie asked with

an inquisitive look on her face. "I'm not sure who you really are and I don't care. I saw you add pills to my father's drink and I'm quite sure they were my pills."

I stand there for a moment because I had no idea anyone saw me crush pills and put them inside Moretti's drink and food. I have to see just how much she knows and is willing to keep to herself. So I apologize immediately and become tearful as I beg for forgiveness to see her response.

"You don't have to apologize to me Nurse Monroe because I don't care.

You do need to be careful, because my mom doesn't trust you. I overheard her talking to my daddy's flunkies and she told them to watch you when she's not here. Just be careful okay? Now I know why he stays in the bed all day," Gabbie says as she chuckles.

"Thanks for looking out for me Gabbie. I know your Mom doesn't trust me because she drilled me when I first got here, and watches me like a hawk," I say.

"Tell me what's the deal with you? Why are you drugging him?" Gabbie inquires.

"Now I have to ask if I can trust you," I respond.

"You most certainly can. Just let me know what I can do to help you."

"Some years ago, your Dad did some awful things to some people and they have asked me to help them repay your father for his evil doings." Over the past months, I've learned to trust Gabbie, even though I've been cautious my entire life. I'm not going to start telling the truth about my family now. In due time, Gabbie will find out the truth—her twins are my husband's niece and nephew. "I'll definitely need you to help me keep an eye out for his flunkies, because if they catch me, I know they will kill me." I ask Gabbie with a softer tone in my voice.

"Don't worry, I got your back," Gabbie assures me.

CHAPTER 18

ONE, TWO PUNCH
SHEILA

Working for Moretti hasn't been as difficult as I thought and I've learned so much from Gabbie about them. Mrs. Moretti continues to watch me like a hawk when she's home, and when she's not, she gets her flunkies to watch me. However, they don't watch me like she does. I don't like her for several reasons, but the main one is she's less than a woman, in my opinion, to allow her grandchildren to be snatched away from their mom's arms. Two, what mother allows their child to be imprisoned in their makeshift dungeon, before being committed to the psych ward.

Not only has Gabbie not seen her children, but also as a grandmother, she hasn't either. Where are her maternal instincts?

After several months, one night on my way home, I'm certain I saw one of Moretti's flunkies is following me. I'm quite sure Mrs. Moretti had him do it because she doesn't have any information about me. I pretend not to see him and stop at the store to buy milk and bread to make it look official. He follows me all the way to our townhouse. I have plenty of weapons inside and a safe room for protection. Once he sees me go inside he pulls off. I place my back against the closed door and take a deep breath. Even though I have weapons here, being followed by his people leaves me with an uneasiness that makes me want to quit now. I know I can't. I'd like to lead some semblance of a normal life. With the rest of my family.

As usual, once I feel the coast is clear, I call my husband to download any intel from the day. He does try to ease my tensions, and probably his, by informing me that Hector is there to look out for me as well.

After speaking with Tony, I call my father to let him know everything was going fine. I asked my father what the plans are for taking the family down?

I have some plans of my own.

There are times that Mrs. Moretti has run out to do errands of her own and Mr. Moretti had no one to go to the bank for him. He didn't trust his flunkies with his money and obviously too drugged up to go himself, so he asks me to deposit money for him. I did this quite a few times and I made sure I brought back the deposit slips to further build his trust in me, which he does for sure now. Out of that trust, his banker assumes that I will be the one to handle his banking if Mrs. Moretti is unavailable. I have all of his account numbers. I text them to both my father and my husband before deleting them out of my phone. With this information, I think we should take all of his money first and then kill him. We got to kill his wife too because I don't like this bitch.

The next day, Gabbie told me that her mom sent one of Moretti's workers out to follow me. That's one reason why I know I can trust her. She lets me know everything that goes on when I'm not here, which is invaluable to me considering her mother is fishing for information on me. For now, all I can do is continue my routine and head up to Moretti's bedroom. I immediately notice that not only is he awake, but he's accompanied by Mrs. Moretti who stops their conversation the moment she sees me.

"Good morning Mr. and Mrs. Moretti. I have your breakfast for you but let me take your vitals before you eat," I say placing a stethoscope on his heart and placing my forefinger and middle finger on his wrist with my free hand. "Your heart is beating extremely fast. Are you okay?" I ask trying to wane some sort of concern even though I could care less.

"I guess it's because of the talk my wife and I just had. I'll be fine. Once I take my meds, I know I will feel better," Moretti assures me.

"I personally don't like that he stays asleep majority of the day. Ever since you've been here, it seems as though my husband is getting worse, not better," Mrs. Moretti says with her arms folded at her chest. She glares at me with her hardened eyes, thinking that shit will intimidate me.

"In my profession, I've notice a lot of patients in your husband's condition tend to sleep a lot. It's okay. It's absolutely normal. There's no need to worry," I say using my profession as my backup. "I will get him out of bed today and walk with him around the house if that will make you feel better." I have to start doing things with Mr. Moretti so she can stop being suspicious. This bitch is getting on my last nerve. Before this is all over, I'm whoopin' her ass!

"Yes, Nurse Monroe, that will make me feel much better. I need to see him out of the bed," Mrs. Moretti agrees.

"Not a problem. As soon as you're done with your breakfast Mr. Moretti, I will give you your meds and then I will get you out of bed and walk with you around the house," I advise Moretti.

Over the next few days, I continue to get Mr. Moretti out of bed, and he seems to be getting back to his normal state. I know I need to start putting those pills in his drink again, but this bitch has been watching my every move. She's even been coming in the kitchen while I prepare his meals. Granted, she's behaving as a normal wife with a strange woman in her home should be behaving in a sense, and that shit is driving me crazy.

Today is the day that I choose to slip some more pills in Moretti's drink. Mrs. Moretti is out today and only three flunkies are in the house. I didn't see my husband's friend, but the three men that were there didn't seem to be watching me as much and Gabbie is upstairs in the shower. I decide to go for it. As soon as start crushing the pills, I hear the clanking of Mrs. Moretti shoes before the shriek in her yell stills my motions. Clearly I've become too at ease because I should have heard her come into the kitchen.

"What the hell are you putting in my husband's glass!" she snaps.

I'm dead.

I know I'm busted and had nothing to say because she visibly knows all his meds and realizes that there's no reason for me to crush whatever it is that I'm giving him. She stares violently at me, her eyes fuming as she awaits an answer. I guess that answer didn't come as soon as she expects because she walks right up to my face and slaps the shit out of me. Before I could stop my motion, I was punching this bitch in her face hard. I hit her with a three-piece so quick she didn't even see it coming. I didn't stop there. All the angst and animosity built over the last few months have found their outlet. Unfortunately for her, it's with my fists. I continue beating the shit out of her. I held her down on the kitchen floor and commenced to whooping her ass. If they are going to kill me at least I get to beat her the fuck up.

She yelled for her flunkies and two big burly men grab me. "She has been drugging my husband. I knew I didn't trust her!" She begins yelling some shit in Italian that sounds like insults making me want to lunge for her more. "Who sent you? Who do you work for?"

The last thing I remember was her telling them to put me in the dungeon.

Gabbie

Since Nurse Monroe has been here this is the first time I've felt as though someone cares for me since my fiancé Phil. She has helped wean me off my meds and genuinely cares about me. My own mother and father seem to hate me, and Nurse Monroe allows me to feel what a mother's love is supposed to feel like. I want out of this house so badly. I feel so alone here and I still feel like a prisoner locked up in my own home.

When I get out of the shower, I know I hear yelling, but I'm unable to decipher the conversation. I quickly dry myself off and throw something on before sneakily walking halfway down the stairs. I see my mom and two of my father's workers dragging Nurse Monroe into the dungeon. She was out cold, the sight of her limp body sending chills throughout my limps as I hope she's only unconscious.

"As soon as this bitch opens her eyes let me know," my mother commands.

The urge to help her overwhelms me enough to get my feet to run and find her purse and phone from the hall closet to hide in my room. No one knows just how close we've become, so I have no doubt they won't come looking for any of her possessions in my room. Besides, most of the people in this house pretend I don't exist. I've never moved so fast throughout this house. I need to do what I can. She's the only person who wants to help me. As I run back to my room, I overhear my mother tell the men to find Nurse Monroe's possessions.

I pretend to be asleep because I didn't want my mom to know I knew anything. Monroe never told me who to call or what to do in this case, but I have to figure out a way to help because I know my father is going to tell them to kill her.

I get up and stand at my doorway and I can hear my mom yelling telling my father she caught Nurse Monroe putting something in his drink and that's probably why he's been sleeping so much and seems to be getting worse. She also tells him that she and Nurse Monroe had a fight. The thought immediately brings a smile to my face.

"Oh, I hope Nurse Monroe beat her ass," I think out loud.

I hear my mother also tell him Monroe is in the dungeon passed out, so she was unable to question her. She's waiting for Giovanni and Leonardo to let her know when Monroe is awake.

I finally hear the roar of my father's voice echo through the house, and much more concise than my mother's. "Who sent this bitch into my home? I want answers now! Where is everyone? I want extra security outside of my house. I feel so stupid letting someone get this close to me and my family! Call Maria and make sure she's okay. Do not alarm her, just check in." He continues shouting rants throughout the house.

It was quiet for a few seconds and then my dad yells out, "If this bitch does not give me the answers I need, I'm going to kill her."

Fear jolts me and I pace back and forth in my bedroom, because I know my father is not playing around. I was so afraid for Nurse Monroe, which I begin to shake. I have to help her.

Okay Gabbie you can do this. Nurse Monroe helped you now it's time to help her.

This is bringing back memories that I'm not sure I can handle. Memories that took me to the darkest of places. Even this dungeon that I know all too well. My parents put me there after my breakdown once my father instructed my sister to kill my fiancé. They thought I was going to tell the police everything, so they locked me in the dungeon after they lied to the police, whom he pays off, and told them that my fiancé killed himself. For good measure, they claim I'm bipolar and commit me into the psych ward.

The dungeon is underneath my bedroom. Through the vents I can hear a faint whisper coming through. It was Nurse Monroe asking for help through soft, labored breaths.

"Somebody help me," she continues to whisper.

I lay my body flat on the floor to get as close to the vents as possible. "Sheila, it's Gabbie. Can you hear me?"

"Gabbie," she coarsely whispers between coughs, "your mom-caught me put-ting pills...dad's drink," she says as if she's having trouble breathing. "She had two men drag me in this dark cave-like room."

I can tell she's afraid as her words become more shaky the more she realizes she's trapped and there's nothing she can do about it. "I know where you are. Those two men are sitting outside the door, so don't talk too loudly. They are going to question you and my father said he was going to kill you," I say.

"Okay Gabbie. Listen to me very carefully. Get my phone and call—Oh my god! They're coming! Help! Help!"

"Oh God...call who?" I whisper hoping she can hear me, but it was too late. The only response I hear is Leo and Gio saying to stop yelling because no one can hear her screams.

At the sound of their voice, I quiet myself as much as possible. There's no way they can know I'm helping her. I take her phone into my bathroom and search through it. She didn't have names stored, only numbers, so I don't know who to call. I get more and more frantic as they continue berating her, asking her questions, followed by a painful blow to her body. I can hear her screams, so I know they are torturing her. I don't know what I should do, and the fact that I can't find a way to help quickly frustrates me more. I panic as her screams become louder, so I cover my ears to try to keep from crying. The screaming finally stops, and I hear the doors close to the dungeon. I hope it's not too late.

I head downstairs to see if I could get some sort of answers. Anything to help me get her some help here quickly. In the kitchen, I see my mom leaning against the counter on her phone. So, I pretend to be drowsy and ask, "what was all the yelling for?"

"Nothing. Go back upstairs," she says in a terse tone.

I suddenly see my father come in, his men following close behind.

"I need answers and I need them now! Go easy on her for now because I'm going to make her answer me before I kill her," he yells at Leo and Gio.

"Gabbie go back upstairs!" Mom yells.

"I'm going mother, but I wanted to get something to eat first," I respond.

I was stalling to see if I could hear anything, so I made two sandwiches with chips and got something to drink. But all I knew for sure is they didn't kill her.

I went upstairs to my room and lay on the floor next to the vent. I tried calling her, but she must be knocked out cold from whatever they did. I kept trying until I heard her gurgling. "Sheila it's me Gabbie. Tell me who to call."

"They-they...are going to kill me," she says through faint cries.

"I know they are, but my dad told them to go easy on you because he wants answers on who sent you here and who you work for. I need you to try and hold out, I'm going to help you. Who do I call? I have your phone."

"Call last number I call," she lazily responds.

"Okay. Hold tight, I'm going to call right now," I try to assure her.

As soon as I went into the bathroom to make the call, they went into the dungeon questioning and beating her all over again.

CHAPTER 19

LOYALTY

TONY

These past few months has been hell on me with my wife working for the devil himself. I've been trying to keep my cool around the girls so they will feel everything is under control. I'm my wife's protector and I don't feel as though I'm protecting her by putting her right in Moretti's arms. The thoughts are driving me crazy of what he will do to my wife if he gains knowledge of her identity.

I'm glad my brother and nephews are here because it's giving me a little solace.

I received a phone call today from Thaddeus Blackman himself. I can't even lie, I was a little too damn excited to be on the phone with *The* Thaddeus Blackman. These aren't the best circumstances to finally have a conversation with my infamous father-in-law. I need to maintain my composure because it must be serious if he's calling me.

"Hello, this is your wife's father." He didn't give me time to say hello or anything. He cut right to the chase, with a stern tone.

"I have a camera hidden in the heart monitor so I can keep an eye on my daughter. It's only visual, I cannot hear what's being said and I didn't see her this morning. I can see when she enters his room and gives him his meds. I can only see in the room where the monitor is placed not throughout the house. I didn't see anything out of the ordinary, but if she does not check in, I'm going in."

Blackman says, careful not to mention any of our names.

I made sure to follow his lead and do the same. "I spoke with her the other night and she told me everything was going as planned and not to worry because he really trusts her," I say trying not to read too much into her father's obvious concern.

"Yea she called me the other night as well and told me the same, but on the days that she works, I can see her when she goes into his bedroom. She should be at work today. I didn't see her this morning at all. I saw him leave out of the bedroom this morning so maybe he just went downstairs before she could come up," Blackman reasons.

"Hold on, I'm actually getting a call from her right now," Thaddeus says slightly relieved.

———————————

Gabbie

"Hi. My name is Gabbie and I have Nurse Monroe's phone. My dad is Francesco Moretti, he has her in the dungeon here in our home and they're torturing her. If you don't hurry they will kill her."

I hurry to tell the caller on the other end and hang up before anyone overhears me.

Since the phone call, I've been trying to keep my ear to the door and not miss whatever my father has planned. I'm the only thing between him harming Sheila and whoever the man is I called saving her. As soon as I hear the doorbell ring, I creep down the stairs to try and hear the conversation my father is having. "Okay guys, I called you all in because I need extra security. I don't know who sent this nurse into my home, but she's been drugging me. I'm guessing that eventually she was going to kill me. My wife walked in on her trying to put something in my drink." The murmurs begin amongst the men wondering who sent her.

"We have her locked in the dungeon and I'm going to get answers by any means necessary!" he shouts.

"Whoever sent her may come looking for her, so I need everyone to be ready when they do," he says.

Between my father's bad heart and my meds that Sheila was giving him he has become a little weak.

"I'm not 100% and as of now, my wife Sofia is in charge. Do I make myself clear?" Moretti instructs.

"I need to lay down, I feel so tired and drained," my father says to no one in particular.

"No worries. I'll take you upstairs Moretti so you can get some rest."

I recognize the voice immediately as Hector. I peek around to see what's going on, not worried that I'll be noticed because I never am. I notice that my father could barely stand on his own two feet. As they approach the stairs, I jog back up to the top floor quickly and peer out of my bedroom door and notice how fragile he looks. Although Hector gets him upstairs quickly, I can tell his heart condition, the stress, and the pills are getting the best of him. I'm sure Hector recognizes the same.

Once they are in the room, I stand at the wall beside the door, careful to listen for any footsteps approaching. Hector helps him in the bed before telling my father that he'll take care of everything downstairs. As he walks back out, I quickly go back to my door and until I hear his voice downstairs before I return to the bottom of the staircase to see if I can get any more information from my mother...or even Hector. At first everything was silent, but not for long. I listen as Hector begins to talk to my mother.

"Are you sure his nurse was drugging him?" Hector questions her as he flirtatiously places his hand on her cheek.

What the fuck?

"Yes. I'm sure. I saw her with my own eyes, crushing pills to put in his drink," she spats as she puts her head down, shyly looking away from his concern.

He swipes an unruly hair behind her ear before replacing the same hand back on her cheek.

"I didn't give her time to answer me because I know he can take pills without a problem. There's no need for her to crush any of his pills. When I asked what she was doing she just stood there and didn't answer me. I slapped her in the face, and she jumped on me, punching me in the face."

He examines her face, lifting her head up completely this time. He sways her head around, surveying the damage from Sheila's fist. Clearly my mother is sleeping with this guy. "I was wondering what happened to you. I thought your husband put those bruises on your face," Hector says, before taking a deep breath. "Do you think it's a good idea to torture her? You will never get answers that way. Your husband is upstairs not feeling well, and he left you in charge. I think there's a better way to handle this and get the answers you want."

Hector slightly rubs her bruises. "Let me get something to clean your face." As he cleans her up, I notice that he's trying awful hard to help someone who has betrayed not only his boss, but apparently the woman he's sleeping with. Why? I can only think of one reason, and that is he must be working with whomever I called earlier for Sheila. I have to be sure though. Finally it seems that mother has agreed with Hector's approach and decides to stop the torturing. As they make their way toward the dungeon where I assume Leo and Gio are still maintaining their post, I jog back up to my room and close and lock the door before I lay against the vent to listen in.

I hear my mother excuse Leo and Gio before she goes in

with Hector. The room is silent at first, and eventually Hector tells my mother to leave out. He may have better leverage over Sheila if they spoke alone. As soon as the door shuts, I hear Hector's voice.

"Hey Sheila, it's me Hector. Your husband's friend." He says I hear a slight whimper escape from her. "I just got here, and they told me what happened. I'm going to help get you out of here and I'm going to call your husband. Try not to tell them anything because once you tell them they will kill you. I will keep them from beating you—you got my word. Even if I have to give myself up for you I will."

Now I know for sure that I can trust Hector.

With that, I hear him walk out of Sheila's prison, but doesn't close the door behind him. He tells the guards there's no need to continue beating her, she's so close to death.

"We don't take orders from you. Who the hell do you think you are?" I hear Gio snap.

"Well, from this point on you will be taking orders from Hector until my Husband is 100 percent." my mother interjects.

I hear the footsteps of who I assume are the guards leaving the dungeon area. It's hard to believe they don't know my mother and Hector has been carrying on an affair. After all, it only took me moments of seeing them together to know.

"Sofia, I think you should go upstairs and check on your husband. He really didn't look good when I took him upstairs. I will go back in here and see if I can get any answers out of her," Hector says.

It seems my mother does what she is told because I hear footsteps leaving the dungeon.

"Tony, it's me Hector. They are on to your wife. They have her in the dungeon and they are torturing her," Hector informs the man quickly.

Unfortunately for him, he doesn't hear the footsteps coming into the dungeon. Whoever is there has heard the entire conversation. I hear what sounds like Hector's phone hitting the floor and then nothing. Then the startling sound of a gunshot makes me jump to my feet as my heart begins to pulsate quickly against my chest. They've killed him. Either way, that phone call alone, accompanied with mine should get them here even faster. I need to find safety.

CHAPTER 20

GET THAT BITCH

IRIE

"Hey M, my cousin Donavan just called and said they are up here chillin' for the weekend. He told me to bring my friends and link up with them," I say.

"Cool because I was bored as fuck," M responds.

"Perfect! Let's get dressed and we're out. He gave me the address to where they will be."

Once we pull up to the house, I call my cousin because I didn't see any cars out front. He instructs me to go in the house because the door should be unlocked. As soon as we get inside, I see Chelsea and Destiny, Zak and Q's cousins. I thought everything was good, but that's definitely not how it feels. That greeting we normally received from family was not what we got at all. In fact, no one even spoke. In the blink of an eye, they jump on M and began to beat the life out of her. I freeze initially, then finally find my footing and try to stop them, but this tall muscular man with a Sunni pulled me away from the brawl, then told me to get in my car and leave. I think momentarily that I have to try and help her, but he gives me a look that scares the living daylights out of me, so I do as I'm told.

As soon as I got back in the car, I called my cousin back

crying. "What the hell is going on? Bombaclat! Dis a crazy waah happenin'?"

"Listen cuddy this is much bigger than you and it has nothing to do with you at all. Her past has come back to haunt her. I know this is your friend, but she gotta pay the price," Donovan says trying to sway my anger.

"That's my friend though, you actually had me set her up. This is fucked up on so many levels. I have to go back in there and help her."

"I'm your cousin and I'm telling you, do not go back in there. Would you have brought her here if I would have just told you what it was about? Nah. You wouldn't have. Don't worry, go back to school and continue your classes. You will be fine. I will explain everything to you later." Donovan hangs up on me.

Oh my God! What am I supposed to do? Do I just leave her in there? Do I go back inside and try to help her? My own cousin is clearly a part of this revenge plot. I would never cross them for anyone, even though M is my friend. I'm so confused. I'm going to call Zak and Q to see if they know what is going on.

I pick up my phone to try and get through to them, but nothing. *Why the fuck are they not answering my call.* Let me try again. My mind immediately thinks they must have something to do with this shit. *Did they set M up?* What reason would they have to set her up? I need answers.

I don't know how I was able to drive back to school. The tears were pouring down my face and my visibility was nonexistent. I got myself together before I exited my car, because I didn't want anyone to see me crying. When I get back in the house, I continue calling Zak and Q's phones, neither answers me.

Why would their cousins jump on M and beat her up? Who the hell was the tall guy with the Sunni? Who's house was that?

Oh my God, I have so many unanswered questions. She is going to hate me. She's always had my back since day one. I don't know what to do or whom to call.

————————————————————

Gabbie

As I lay on the floor listening through the vents I can hear my mother's footsteps entering the dungeon and she begins to question my dad's flunkies.

"Did our nurse give you any information?" Mom asks.

"No, she didn't but your boy toy did," Giovanni says as they both snicker.

Oh so maybe the flunkies do know Mom is sleeping with Hector.

"What the hell are you talking about Giovanni?" She asked harshly.

"When we walked inside to see if Hector got any information out of her, we overheard him on the phone with someone named Tony, telling him that they are on to his wife and they are torturing her. So, we shot and killed his ass for being a traitor," Giovanni pleads.

"Nooo!" Mom yells.

I can hear my mom's footsteps quickly running through the dungeon. Her piercing screams rang through the vent, which lets me know she witnessed Hector's body lying dead on the floor.

"This can't be true. Why would you betray me!" I hear my mother yelling through her tears. I hear my mom run out of the dungeon yelling and screaming, "Get the fuck out of my house! Both of you are fucking fired you morons. Get out now!"

I get up off the floor and proceed to my bedroom door so I

can hear them clearly and I hear the flunkies leaving and mom running upstairs to tell my dad that Tony Davis is the one who sent the nurse here to kill him.

"Phil's brother Tony?" My dad questions with skepticism in his voice.

"Yes! That Tony. You were right about Hector. He was betraying us.

Leonardo and Giovanni overheard him on the phone talking to Tony. They said he told Tony that they are on to his wife. I didn't know Tony had a wife," Mom says while throwing her lover under the bus.

"Bring Leo and Gio up here now so I can ask them questions about what else they heard him say," Dad requests.

"I just fired them both and threw them out of the house." Mom states harshly.

"Why the hell would you do that Sofia?" My father scolds.

"Those two morons didn't get any info from him before they killed him. I asked them and the only thing they heard was a short conversation. How are they just going to kill the enemy without asking questions?" She says, "That's the reason we haven't killed the nurse yet. We need answers!" Mom drives her reasoning into my dad so he wouldn't become suspicious of her actions. "I asked them if they were working with Hector. I also asked them if they silenced him before he told on them. They couldn't answer, so I dismissed them."

My mom had to make it believable to my dad because she's aware that Leo and Gio knows that Hector is her lover. Mom's afraid they will tell my dad so that's the real reason she got rid of them.

"Good job honey! I knew you could handle things whenever I needed you to. I'm not sure what they are talking about because I know Tony doesn't have a wife. Let's go downstairs and get answers from this bitch," Dad says.

For Dad to be such a boss he's such a sucker for my mom.

I ran downstairs top speed before my parents could even get out of their bedroom. I didn't see anyone in sight, which was very strange. I could still hear mom and dad talking in their bedroom, so I walked to the dungeon, quickly noticing that no one was guarding the door. I peeked through the door, but nobody was guarding the inside either. I walked down the hall of the dungeon and I saw Hector lying on the floor in a pool of blood. I had to get myself together because he reminded me of my fiancé, lying in his own blood.

You can do this Gabbie. That's not Phil lying there. Sheila needs help. I quickly shook my head to remove the horrible memories.

I looked over and noticed Nurse Monroe was still alive and crying. When she looked up and saw me, there was a little relief in her eyes.

"Gabbie help me. Untie me." Sheila asks through her pained mouth.

I hurried to untie her before anyone showed up. Sheila bends over the guy lying in blood. She checks his neck to see if he has a pulse.

"He tried to help me, and they heard him on the phone with my husband, and they shot and killed him. He was my husband's friend." Sheila says through her tears.

"I got to get out of here before they kill me too. I know my people are far away. By the time they get here I might be dead already."

"Gabbie did you bring my purse and cell phone?"

"No, it's hidden in my room. I didn't think I was going to be able to get in here to see you. I wasn't expecting the door to be unguarded. My parents are upstairs in their bedroom talking about him." I explained to her as I pointed to Hector's body lying on the floor.

"I'm going with you, I hate it here. Let me go upstairs and get your purse and phone."

"No! No! You may get caught. Let's just get out of here now," she says.

"Ok we can go out the back door I don't want us to get caught from the men my father has out front guarding the house."

"It's going to take us a while to get to the streets for help. It's like a mile from here," I inform her.

"I don't care. I'd rather take my chances out there than to stay here and get killed," she insists.

Sofia

We went down to the dungeon to try and get answers from the nurse, but we knew something was wrong once we noticed the door is open to the dungeon. As soon as we stepped inside, we realized the nurse was gone. Someone helped her because the ties were lying on the floor. I know she didn't untie herself. *What the fuck is going on?*

"Who else is a traitor?" Moretti shouts.

"**Gabbie!**" I ran upstairs and sure enough, Gabbie was gone. I searched her room and found Nurse Monroe's purse and phone underneath her mattress along with pills that she pretended to take. My husband follows me upstairs to Gabbie's room and I show him the nurse's purse and cell phone and Gabbie's pills.

"Gabbie's been helping her?" My husband asks with venom in his voice.

"Everyone has betrayed me! She's dead to me," My husband shouts.

We went back to our bedroom. My husband calls one of his guards who is guarding the front of the house.

"My daughter Gabbie and the nurse have escaped. They are on foot so go out there, find them and bring them back to me," Moretti commands, before he could answer my husband we hear gunshots ring through the phone.

"They're here." My husband yells.

My husband and I hide inside our safe room located inside my walk-in-closet. They wouldn't be able to find us in here. We hear them kick in our front door, which means they must have killed all of my men out front. We look through the cameras from inside the safe room and turn on the intercom so we can hear them. We see about eight men with guns and one of them was the infamous Tony Davis, the others I didn't recognize, but one of the men wore a ski mask and gloves.

"Tony come with me. Jamar you'll stand guard. When the daughter called me, she said they took her to the dungeon," The one with the ski mask says to them.

I look at my husband and say, "Gabbie called them."

The other men stood guard throughout my house while Tony and the ski mask man went searching for our dungeon. Tony and the ski mask man returned after their search for Tony's wife obviously came up short.

"We found the dungeon, but my wife is gone." Tony tells the other men.

"They killed my friend Hector. He called me and they over-heard him on the phone. He was truly a loyal friend. He risked his life for my wife. I know I have to make sure his family is well taken care of." Tony continues.

My husband shakes his head and says, "I knew Hector was a traitor, but I never thought in a million years he was helping Tony Davis. While I was plotting to kill Tony and his brother, he was plotting to kill me."

We continue listening to Tony and his goons through our intercom.

"Maybe the daughter that called you helped her. I gotta find my wife before Moretti finds her. Now that he knows she's my wife, he will kill her for sure. Let's go! I know these bougie ass neighbors heard the gun shots and called the cops by now." Tony says.

CHAPTER 21

WAR
MORETTI

M y wife and I waited to come out of the safe room until we were sure Tony and his goons left.

"Let's go! We don't have time to get anything."

I'm so glad I took my lover's word of advice to get another house. Even though it was going to be for Zakkiyah, desperate times call for desperate measures. I know my wife is going to question me about the house, I'll just tell her it was going to be a surprise for her.

Once we get to my other house, I called more of my trusted soldiers to meet me there. I sent two of them out to look for Nurse Monroe and my daughter. I also sent them a picture of my daughter to their phones and told them to bring them to me. Nurse Monroe is wounded terribly so they couldn't get too far. They are probably still in the area of my house.

———————————————

Gabbie

"GABBIE I NEED to sit down. My entire body is aching, and I know I have some broken bones. I just need a minute to rest." Nurse Monroe says.

"Okay we can sit right here for now but it's really cold. We can't stay out here for long. We don't have a coat or anything," I say.

"Stay here Sheila and I will try and make it to the road and get help," I say anxiously.

As soon as I made it to the streets, I saw a truck driving slowly down the road. I flagged it down. When they stopped, I noticed it was two men in the truck. At first, I was nervous but they were not any of my daddy's flunkies that I've ever seen before so I told them my friend needs help can they please assist us. With no hesitation, they walked with me back to the area where I left Nurse Monroe.

Once there, one of the men picked her up and carried her back to the truck. He told me to sit in the front while the other one sat in the back with Nurse Monroe. I asked them to take us to the nearest hospital because she needs a doctor. I really didn't know which way the hospital was because I don't get out much. When he pulled up in front of an unfamiliar house, I knew something was wrong. I question where we were and neither of the men said a word. Two more men came out and grabbed me and hauled me inside and the other men carried Nurse Monroe.

Unfortunately when we got inside of the house, we were facing the devil himself. My father..

"So, my own daughter betrayed me!" He yells.

"You and mother dearest have ruined my entire life. You all go on with your lives and leave me stuck in the house drugged up on those pills," I yell back.

"Pills that you no longer take," My mom says sternly.

I shoot her a look to kill and for the first time my mother shuts her mouth.

"I have kids that are 8 years old and I've never laid eyes on them because of you. You don't care what you have done to me and yet you think I care about betraying you. I hate all of you! I don't care if you kill me, I have nothing to live for, thanks to you." I scream.

As I'm yelling at my parents we hear Nurse Monroe's phone ringing. My dad answers her phone and places it on speaker for everyone to hear.

"Tony my friend. Is that you? Did you really think you could send your precious wife in my home to kill me and I not find out who she is? Are you crazy? You might as well say your good-byes because you will never see her again. I will continue to torture her and let it be a slow painful death. Plus, I'm still going to kill you and your brother, because I know you have my money," My dad says in his devilish voice.

"Say hello to your husband for the last time."

"I love you babes. It's okay, I did this for my family," Sheila says through clinched teeth.

"Don't worry we are coming to get you," Tony assures her.

"Okay that's enough! Remember Tony, I'm going to kill you and I'll bury you next to your wife. At least you'll be together again," My dad says.

"If you kill my wife Moretti, I will kill everyone in your family. Starting with your precious daughter."

"I don't know how you will do that because my daughter is right here with me. Oh yeah, she tried helping your wife, and you see how that turned out."

"Oh no Moretti, not your daughter Gabbie, your daughter Maria. M is what they call her right?" Tony says slyly.

My dad becomes so quiet over the phone, it's as if he stopped breathing or something.

"Are you still there Moretti?" Tony asks.

My dad looks like someone hit him in the chest with a ton of bricks. He grabs his head and sweat profusely.

"You don't have my daughter Tony. My daughter is safe and sound," he looks over at my mom and she gave him a look of uncertainty. Tony hangs up on my dad.

"Call Maria's phone now!" My dad shouts to my mom.

"It's going straight to voicemail," Mom says nervously.

"Keep trying! And trying! Until you get her!" My dad continues to shout.

Nurse Monroe starts laughing, so my dad punches her in the face.

"You should have a seat before you have another heart attack," Nurse Monroe teases through an obvious fractured jaw.

"Just remember, whatever you do to me, my husband will do to your precious daughter Maria...or M is it?" She snickers as she makes a hardy laugh avoiding the pain best as she can considering the pain she's obviously in.

Nurse Monroe's phone begins to buzz and when my dad looked at it, he saw several pictures of my sister, his precious Maria. Her face is beat up, eyes swollen shut, with blood running down the side of her head.

This is war!

To be continued...

ACKNOWLEDGMENTS

Thank you, God, for giving me a creative mind to become an author. Thank you for keeping me well enough to complete this task. You get all the honor and the praise.

There are two people I would like to acknowledge for sticking by me through this writing journey:

My loving and supportive spouse, Terrance Shelton, I would like to thank you for believing in me when I didn't believe in myself. You pushed me past my breaking point and encouraged me to stay the course. *I love you, Mr. Shelton.*

My daughter, Ajee', you are my wardrobe manager, my "Lingo" fact-checker, and critic. You keep me young at heart. You are my one and only; My miracle. *I love you, Poo.*

Other acknowledgments:

Daa'iyah Harris- Executive Assistant
Jelani Joseph- Photographer
Kendell Dempster- MUA
Alzhane McMillion-Nichols- Fashion Designer
Keke Thompson- Hair stylist

My book cover models:

Ajee' Shelton
Ayanna Rabb
Chanel Wells
Jelani Harris

Special Thanks:

To Author Cam Johns,

Thank you for taking me under your wing in such a short period of time and pushing me to become a better writer. I'm forever grateful for your mentorship.

KeKe Thompson, hair specialist at Illtown Salon.

-love, nicole

ABOUT THE AUTHOR

Nicole Horn-Shelton was born and raised in Newark, New Jersey. She now resides in Elizabeth, New Jersey. She is married to the love of her life Terrance Shelton. They share their only child Ajee'. Nicole retired at the early age of 44 but not truly ready to stop working so she decided to work on her goals. Nicole has been inspired to write since she was a child. Her imagination is extensive and forever thinking of ways to make things better.

She is an enthusiastic, passionate and humorous writer. Her creative mind is phenomenal and will take her readers on an emotional journey.

The writing process behind her book has been a long road and she is ready and eager to share with the world. This book is like her second baby and she has nurtured it as such. Her writing is created to put you in the characters' shoes.

Made in the USA
Columbia, SC
19 June 2022